I0671659

Jonathan Sturak

Clouded
Rainbow

A NOVEL

PENDAN PUBLISHING

Revised 2nd Edition

Published in the United States of America by Pendan Publishing

The Library of Congress has catalogued the paperback edition as
follows:
Sturak, Jonathan
Clouded Rainbow : A Novel
p. cm.
ISBN: 978-0-9825894-0-3

www.sturak.com

To You

Clouded
Rainbow

One word frees us of all the weight and pain of life:
that word is love.
~Sophocles

1

A BATTERED MAN WANDERS IN THE POURING RAIN. He is tall and wears an expensive black suit that is drenched with the sky's tears. His footsteps splash on the cold, hard ground as he staggers down the center yellow line of the city street. It is night and, although tall glass-encased buildings fill the metropolis and mirror the brilliant streetlights, the city is lifeless. Not a car, a person, or an animal fills the sprawling downtown. There are only two living beings—the man and the rain. His eyes are wide open as the water traverses his day old stubble. He is a man on a mission. The water pelts his fragile frame as his dark hair expels liquid like a drenched sponge. A flash of lightning and a clash of thunder echo through the overwhelming structures, but the man does not flinch. He continues toward somewhere that only he knows. As his steps seem to lead nowhere, a glimmer of something comes into his view. It is subtle yet definite and seems to complement the man's drive. As the lights grow closer, they separate into two distinct headlights. At first, it appears as though the vehicle is a police sedan of some sort, but as the lights split farther apart, the identity of the vehicle reveals itself as a screaming tractor-trailer.

The creature devours the road as its powerful V-12 engine inhales all in its path like a ferocious lion searching for its next prey. Like the king of the jungle, this beast is the king of the roadway. The windows are blacked out and the driver is unknown. It is as if the vehicle is driving on sheer hunger. Its roaring engine overtakes the sound of the rain as its jaws maintain perfect precision with the endless yellow line.

The unresponsive man continues on his journey. His eyes maintain focus straight ahead at the encroaching force, but he does not blink. It is as if he has no worries, no fear, and no pain. Something is motivating the man to continue down the deadly path—something incomprehensible, something in his determined eyes. A slight yet distinctive glow in his dilated pupils proves his force. Suddenly, another flicker reflects in the whites of his eyes. This sparkle, however, is not part of the man's determination, but part of the high beams speeding his way.

The truck is within a hundred yards of the determined traveler. Both stick to the yellow line like two chugging trains forced onto the same track. Abruptly, the man stops cold. His eyes remain wide but deep red blood begins to ooze from the orifice. The truck consumes the yards between them. Fifty...forty...thirty. The monster blares its horn. The man takes his last breath and mouths the word "dynamite."

A calm silence filled the office as Roger Belkin sprang awake at his desk. He rarely dozed off on his throne, but today he felt unusually tired. Roger was a handsome man ripened to the age of thirty-five. He was tall with dark features where it counted and parted his hair to the side in a 1950s style. Roger enjoyed this time of the day. It was four o'clock, and he only had thirty minutes left at work. It wasn't that he disliked his job, but he was swept up in the anticipation of spending the rest of the evening with his wife. In fact, his job was exactly what he wanted to do after college. Following high school, he was accepted to his first choice school, Penn State. It wasn't the party atmosphere or venerable football history that drew him; it was the tradition. His grandfather attended the university to study business management, and his father graduated from there after studying economics. It was fitting that Roger took the baton and acquired his higher education from the school in "Happy Valley."

The businessman's forte was in the stock market, the almighty dollar, and ways that investors could reap the benefits of big business. The stock market allowed the average Joe with a computer, some research skills, and business sense to rake in big bucks easily. This was something instilled in Roger during his tenure at Penn State and reaffirmed with a glance at his degree in finance, which hung proudly on his office wall.

Roger's watch read three minutes past four, which jarred his attention. He always seemed to forget about his office pet, Guppy the fish. Guppy was an office gift from his secretary a few months ago. At first, he feared the burden of feeding the scaly creature. But after a few days, he looked forward to it. The fish was a brilliant bluish green. It swam around in a small bowl lined with rocks, simulated green weeds, and an arched sign that read "Beware." He let his secretary handle the weekly water changes, but Roger never missed its daily feeding. On weekends, though, he usually wasn't at the office. However, the fish food market had solved that problem. They invented food tablets that lasted varying amounts of time, including a two-day weekend.

Today, the fish seemed a bit sluggish and not its usual self. Roger grabbed the food pellets and carefully held back his suit coat in order to protect his three hundred dollar jacket. As the pellets hit the water, the fish thrust to the surface and inhaled the specks.

Roger's desk phone buzzed. The noise startled him.

"Mr. Belkin, I have Dr. Kim on line one," his secretary said.

Roger took a moment to think. Dr. Kim was his family doctor, but he considered him to be more of his wife's doctor than his. Roger was terrified of medicine. He had a subconscious fear of death, which he never expressed—not even to his life partner. He was terrified of not only the mere fact of dying, but also of the unknown realm that would face him after he had taken his last breath. Out in the world, he tucked the fear into the deepest part of his brain and did his best to keep it there. However, in a doctor's office, or even worse, a hospital, life and death were everywhere. It baffled him how doctors treated life like a machine, usually following procedures to diagnose an ailment by consulting a reference manual like a mechanic checking a vehicle repair handbook. Dr. Kim was a decent man, and a generous financial client of his, but Roger always felt a hint of defensiveness when he talked to him.

Finally, Roger chimed back, "Thank you, I'll take it now."

"Hi, Dr. Kim. How are you, sir?" Roger asked cheerfully.

"Very well, Roger. So when are you coming to see me? I've been waiting for you to schedule an appointment. If you don't do it for yourself, at least do it for your wife."

The doctor's reference to his wife put a grin on his face. "I know doc. I'll have to put that on my list. Lois has been pushing me about that too."

"Which list is that? The same list that your father forgot to keep?"

"What is this call referring to?" Roger asked.

"My apologies, Roger. I shouldn't have said that. How is Lois? I hope she is well."

"Yes, always keeping me on my toes. I don't know what I'd do without her," Roger replied with another grin.

"I'm calling for some investment advice. I know that health care is booming. I should know because the practice here is doing quite well."

"Yes, with the baby boomer population aging, the health care industry is garnering the financial benefits. Pharmaceuticals are a hot sector. Several big names had record earnings this past quarter, beating market estimates."

"I'm thinking of investing in a good health care mutual fund. What do you think?" the doctor asked.

"Great decision, sir. I would be happy to prepare some information for you to review. We are here to take care of our clients. And you, sir, are one of our best," Roger responded as he jotted down a note on his desk pad under "to do."

"Thank you, Roger."

"You're welcome. I'll be in touch with some literature."

"Very well. Talk to you soon," Dr. Kim replied.

Roger said goodbye. Silence returned to his office. He glanced at his watch and saw it read fifteen minutes after four. He knew it was too close to quitting time and simply didn't feel like preparing anything for the doctor. He reasoned with himself that he would take care of that task first thing in the morning. Roger's evening with his wife consumed his mind as the anticipation of a night of lust aroused his senses. He anxiously tapped his foot as he pondered his drive home and the shower he needed to wash the day away before the evening could begin.

Roger stood and scanned his surroundings. When he got his promotion to Investment Manager last year, he couldn't believe the size of his new office. But now that he saw it day after day, it really didn't faze him. He was grateful for it, but something inside him was not impressed. He had always known that he'd get the comfortable office and eager secretary eventually, and when it happened, he wasn't fully satisfied. The one thing, however, that did astound Roger was his exquisite view of the city. When he felt he needed a break or when he was mulling over something in his mind, he would simply stand and take a gander out the window. Looking out from the twenty-fifth floor gave him a feeling of power and dominance. Today was particularly sunny, with only a hint of clouds looming in the blue sky. As Roger paused for a moment at the view, he could see the bustling streets filled with cars and pedestrians moving around downtown. The one thing he wished the view included was the restaurant and bar district near Fourth Street. That was the side of the downtown where he shared the most romantic memories with his wife.

Roger's phone buzzed again. For a moment, his contented grin changed to an angered sneer, but his secretary's words soon brightened his expression, "Mr. Belkin, your wife is on line one."

Roger thought a call from his wife was the best way to conclude his long day. Lois was the love of his life. She and Roger had met at a quaint coffee shop on College Avenue at Penn State. Roger frequented the establishment when he was studying for his business exams or reviewing *The Wall Street Journal*. Then one evening, she stepped into his life—a tall, glowing woman with a certain aura about her. Roger remembered how he saw her floating through the line and hoped she would sit next to him. Although Roger was an affable man who was always ready with the right thing to say in a business meeting, he was nervous around women. It was fitting that Lois made the first move. She was one year ahead of Roger, a senior to his junior standing. She was a creative writing major with a love for the fine arts. Her parents were extremely affluent. Since she and her sister Carol were their sweet "baby girls," they took care of both sisters financially. Lois liked Roger's boyish looks. His 1950s hairstyle and dimples immediately piqued her attention. Roger and Lois hit it off and dated for two years until Lois, not Roger, popped the question. She always motivated the businessman and took charge in the relationship, but she still let Roger appear to be the alpha male. She let him dominate in the bedroom, where she liked to be a submissive female. Roger and Lois were married for eleven years, had a nice house in the suburbs, and lived close to her older sister Carol. The next logical step, albeit delayed, was having a family. Lois wanted to wait until she was thirty-seven. She did the math and wanted her kids to graduate high school and college when she and Roger were in their fifties. She was born when her mother and father were both twenty-two. Having parents in their thirties when one was going to the prom seemed too close for comfort. She couldn't imagine having gangly teenagers around the house when her teenage years seemed as if they were yesterday. That's why she thought fifty would be ideal. Roger was indifferent. He loved Lois with all of his heart. To him, she was a diamond in the rough among women. He couldn't fathom a world without his wife by his side. He would do anything to provide for her.

Roger sat down and answered his phone with zest. "Hi, honey. How's my little dynamite?"

"Hi, dear. Just checking to see how your day's going," she responded with a smile.

"Not too bad. Just finishing up some end-of-the-month spreadsheets. Hey, I just spoke with Dr. Kim."

"Oh, did he mention—"

"Yeah. He mentioned it again. I think I'll pass on the physical," he responded firmly.

"Ah, you're paranoid. Just get a check-up. Everyone goes regularly after thirty."

"I know, but something about the whole thing just makes me uneasy. If I ever end up in the hospital, make sure you smuggle me out," he chuckled.

"Will you be home on time today?"

Roger smiled, happy to announce that he was just about to walk out the door.

"Yes, dear. Things are pretty quiet around here today. Don't worry. We'll make it this time. I promise."

"I hope so," she replied.

Lois finished the conversation with an update on her daily writing progress. She was writing a novel about a love triangle. Lois free-lanced since college writing restaurant reviews, children's short stories, and film critiques. Her focus for the past year, however, was on the novel. She was nearly finished revising the second draft.

"See you at five, dear. I love you," Roger replied.

"I love you too," Lois responded.

Roger hung up and sat for a moment in his placid office. He glanced at his watch and saw it was four thirty.

Another day down, he thought.

Roger stood up and put his papers in his briefcase. He grabbed something hidden inside his desk, pushed his chair in, and then left his office. As Roger shut the door, he left the room in complete silence. But something on his desk was definitely not right. The beta fish was swimming more slowly. Its usually quick movements had turned sluggish. It moved inch by inch, and then suddenly stopped. The fish held its pose, but then turned belly up, as life drained from the creature.

2

Roger commanded his SUV on the ride home. He couldn't drive anything else as he craved sitting up high and the feeling of protection the brawny machine yielded. Traffic was dense, which was typical for this time of day. As he drove, he glanced down at a picture of him and his wife that he kept on the dashboard. Whenever he checked his speed, staring back at him was Lois on one of their annual excursions to San Francisco. Roger updated the picture after each year's trip to keep the memories fresh.

Up ahead was the Pleasant Place Bridge, a tremendous structure leading in and out of the downtown city. It was relatively close to the water—only about twenty feet above. The bridge was the only way to reach his house, except for another one some fifteen miles on the east side of the city. Sometimes the bridge was backed up, but it was undoubtedly quicker to wait it out than to battle urban traffic on the distant detour.

All at once, pellets of hail pelted the roof of the SUV. Roger flinched for a second as the noise caught him off guard.

That's odd, they said it was supposed to be nice this evening.

As he questioned the weathermen, rain consumed his vehicle. He reached for the windshield wiper knob and turned it just in time. Roger began to cross the bridge but noticed something odd. The water below violently swayed and chopped in a chaotic pattern. It was as if it were alive and yelling, using the wild waves as its voice. Roger took another glimpse of the picture on his dashboard and thought, *I'll be home soon.*

Ten minutes later, the door to Roger's home opened. He ran in from the torrential rain, ducking under his umbrella. Roger checked his briefcase and coat. He hated getting his suits wet because he never heard the end of it from Lois, who was the one who had to get them cleaned and pressed. His solution was stockpiling umbrellas and hiding them in all sorts of places to hopefully stumble upon during a downpour. Actually, it was Lois' suggestion, but Roger was glad for her willingness to help his memory.

"Honey, I'm home," he yelled with a grin.

"I'm in the kitchen, dear," she replied.

Roger left his soiled umbrella on a carpeted area to protect the hardwood floors. Polishing the part in his hair, he walked into the kitchen to greet his wife. As he entered the large, open space, he looked for her to his right and swept his eyes until finally resting on her familiar frame. Roger rarely looked for his wife like this, but today was different. Her flowing brown hair, tall curvy figure, and radiating skin captivated him like the first time he had watched her glide through that coffee shop. Like fine wine resting gently in the protection of a cellar, her feminine qualities seemed to get even more enticing as time gracefully aged them. Roger walked behind her and noticed she was trimming a flower in her hand. He nuzzled his head into the supple skin of her neck as her familiar scent filled his nostrils with bliss. It caused him to savor the moment, a moment he wished could last forever. Lois showed him the beautiful floral arrangement she had been creating on the kitchen counter. Daisies, tulips, and lilacs filled a glass vase offering a colorful mixture of vegetation. She turned from his advancement and touched her soft lips against his, which gave him a taste of the night to come. In the background, the pouring rain outside the kitchen window caught his attention.

"Wow, the rain seems to be even worse now," he remarked with a squint to his eyes.

"I know. I was outside before in the sun picking these. I was chatting with our neighbor while she was hanging clothes."

Roger looked at the neighbor's clothes flapping in the rain. "Her clothes should be dry soon," he sarcastically replied.

"I didn't even know it was supposed to rain today," she responded.

"I'm going to grab a quick shower," Roger said.

"What about the lightning? Don't shower when it rains."

"That's an old wives' tale. I'll be fine."

"Well, we better leave by six fifteen if we want to make it on time. You never know with traffic," Lois lectured.

He pointed to the clock on the wall. It read twenty-five minutes after five.

"See, I made it home before five thirty today. We should be right on time," Roger rebutted.

"You're on the ball, mister," Lois said as she put the finishing touches on the floral arrangement.

"Tonight I will wine, dine, and shine you," he wryly responded. Then, he added a wink.

"You better make sure that shower's a cold one."

Roger leaned in and kissed her tenderly, the way a man did who was infatuated with his sweetheart.

"I love you so, so much, Lois," he whispered as he looked deep into her brown eyes.

"Don't overdo it because it's our—"

He squeezed her tighter. Lois melted.

"I love you more," Lois whispered.

Moments later, Roger hung his head low under the showerhead. The hot water invigorated his senses and rejuvenated his face from the long day at work. Thoughts of the approaching night with his wife floated through his mind.

Roger stepped out into the steamy bathroom, which resembled a sauna at the country club. He dabbed his renewed skin with a towel, and then stood in front of the clouded mirror. He gave the glass a swipe with his hand, which revealed his masculine body. He secretly enjoyed studying his robust frame, even if it sounded vain. Roger analyzed his pectoral muscles camouflaged with just the right amount of hair. He followed a droplet of water with his eyes, and his senses, as it slid chaotically down his abdomen and detoured down his right leg.

Roger towel dried his body and quickly shaved his five o'clock shadow, removing a few years of perceived age. Lois always enjoyed touching his face after a shave and petting the smooth, hairless skin of his cheek.

When Roger stepped out from the bathroom into their master bedroom, Lois' stunning figure in a matching set of black bra and panties provoked him.

"Mmmm," he mouthed. She giggled and gave him a little shake of the hips, which only further ignited the animal inside him.

"Hurry up and get dressed," she playfully instructed.

Roger dressed on his side of the room. When they bought the house, the colossal master bedroom immediately drew them in and drove the couple to shell out the ten percent of the half-million dollar asking price.

Roger fitted himself with a vintage black Hugo Boss 1960-styled suit complemented by a pair of polished leather dress shoes, size eleven. Underneath he wore a tailored dress shirt with a French collar and cuff links. Roger only bought tailored shirts as he hated the excessive material that always fluffed out from the pants. Nothing beat the conforming fabric that accented his perfectly maintained thirty-four inch waist. While Roger put the final additions on his black & white patterned tie, Lois applied lipstick and dabbed perfume on strategic areas of her body.

"Did you talk to your sister today?" Roger asked.

"Yeah, she was happy we sent her the card," Lois replied.

Immediately, a knot tightened in Roger's belly. "Oh, that's right!"

Lois shook her head and frowned. "I knew you'd forget. I bought a card at the store on Monday when I picked up those steaks we had for dinner."

"I would have remembered. Today is only Wednesday," Roger replied in an attempt to cover his forgetfulness, but he only dug himself deeper into a hole of mortification.

"Yeah and today is Carol's birthday. She wouldn't have received the card if I hadn't sent it yesterday."

Her response puzzled him. Roger had a horrible time remembering birthdays, which obviously wasn't out of the ordinary for him. He probably messed this up year after year, and a similar conversation likely occurred this time last year—but, of course, he couldn't remember it!

"I thought tomorrow was her birthday, the twenty third?"

"No, her birthday is the twenty second. Today. Wednesday. My mom's was the twenty third."

Before Roger could fire some brain neurons, the phone blared. Lois answered it. It was Carol, the elusive birthday girl. She was a woman most men would only look at once in public. She was two years older than Lois and had some of the same features, but not enough to warrant a man's second look. The one big difference between the sisters was one of emotion. While Lois was head strong, independent, and educated, Carol was more emotional and conservative. She would cry at weddings and wouldn't mind showing it. Nevertheless, Carol enjoyed playing big sister; she called Lois just about every day to check in. Lois didn't mind; she loved Carol. Lois still felt like the little third grader protected by her sister, the shielding fifth grader.

"Oh. Hi, Carol. Roger and I were just getting ready for our date," Lois said cheerfully.

"How romantic. I wish Robert would take notes," Carol replied with a smile on her face. She was preparing an appetizer for dinner, a green salad for her and her husband, Robert, who was an overworked tax accountant.

"Hi, Carol. Happy Birthday!" Roger yelled with an exaggerated smile. Lois shook her head.

"Oh, tell him thanks for remembering. Again, I loved the card you guys sent."

"I'll be *sure* to tell him," Lois replied sarcastically.

"Well, I'll let you go. I just wanted to see if you were still going because of the bad weather. They say it's one of the worst storms of the season. Just came from nowhere," Carol gingerly explained.

Carol's words made Lois think for a moment. She wondered whether they should go. Lois glanced at Roger as he straightened his tie; the image pacified her.

"We're taking Roger's SUV, so I think we should be fine," she responded.

"Okay, well enjoy. You guys have fun tonight," Carol added.

This put a smile on Lois' face.

"Don't worry, we will. Bye, sis," Lois replied.

As soon as she hung up, she locked eyes with the love of her life. He was standing in his polished suit, looking irresistible. As much as she looked forward to leaving, a part of her couldn't wait to get back.

Roger smiled and simply said, "Ready?"

3

The setting sun burned through the rain clouds. The weather changed abruptly from gloom to bliss before nightfall would engulf the city. Roger steered his SUV across the Pleasant Place Bridge as he admired the rather calm water.

"I guess the storm is over," he said to Lois.

Both were listening to a classical CD. It was part of a master collection of two hundred classic themes from yesterday performed by today's modern orchestras. Beethoven's Seventh Symphony softly echoed inside the vehicle. The couple loved to listen to music without vocals. Lois was particularly fond of being chauffeured around while lying back on the cushioned seat with classical piano melodies resonating in her ears. She had a contented smile on her face as she watched Roger cross the bridge. Up ahead, tall skyscrapers glistened from the angled sun's warming rays. A bounced glimmer caught Roger's eyes; he lowered his visor. The drive was all too familiar to Roger, as it was his way into his office every morning. The major difference was that he usually drove with the sun at the opposite, less-blinding angle. He saw his building for a moment and tried to pick out his window on the twenty-fifth floor, but the turn to the concealed restaurant district prompted a shuffle of the wheel.

As Roger drove, the city transformed from work to play. Couples trekked to the various restaurants and eateries. Business professionals seeking a happy hour retreat walked in and out of the pubs on the corners. Lois was quiet, which was normal for her. Just her simple presence in the car was all that mattered to Roger. He turned periodically toward her to catch a glimpse of her dark dress conforming to her body. He also received a fresh hint of her subtle perfume. As they turned on "Fourth Street," the establishment came into view. Roger could see the sign towering over the road, "The Hideaway."

Outside, several valet drivers scurried, parking the high-end vehicles of the arriving patrons. Lois always liked the feeling of attuned service performed by the usually eager valet staff. She enjoyed giving the typical twenty-something men something to ogle as she swung her exposed legs to the ground.

Roger shifted the SUV into park, took out a folded ten-dollar bill, and then slipped it to the college-aged attendant who greeted the arriving couple.

"Hey, thank you, sir," the young man replied with a smile.

With Lois on his arm, the pair walked inside. The place was more than simply a five-star restaurant and lounge; it was a posh hotel offering guests the very finest in artistic luxury with classic artwork scattering the dimly lit hallways. Full size replicas of the famous works of Van Gogh and Rembrandt, to name a few, greeted the curious clientele. Artwork was even hidden on the ceiling, surprising a guest when he or she had least expected it. The hotel aspect allowed the restaurant to stay open twenty-four hours offering meals, snacks, and appetizers to the refined guests or hungry travelers. Liquor, however, was only served until the two o'clock morning cut off, re-opening when the hour hand struck seven. Despite that, a four a.m. shrimp cocktail or even a full-course meal was available, delivered by the eager restaurant staff.

Roger and Lois walked past Munch's *The Scream* toward the restaurant as the cool, filtered air hit Roger's clean-shaven face. Lois immediately widened her eyes to take in the dimmer lights.

"This gets fancier every time we come," she said to Roger.

The layout was all about simple seclusion. There were three levels of floor, which gave one an ant's eye view of the upper levels when walking in. Large candles lined the walls on both sides of the entryway and provided a feeling that one was entering the confines of a cavern. Servers, dressed only in black, bustled around and seemed to navigate the darkness with ease. Behind a podium was a cute hostess in her twenties. She wore a black outfit with just enough cleavage to force a smile from an approaching male, who usually was the one doing the talking.

"Good evening. Do you have a reservation?" she cheerfully asked.

"Yes. Should be under Belkin," Roger responded.

She glanced in her book, but the glance turned into a stare.

"Um, I'm sorry, sir. I don't see your name. When did you book your reservation?"

"I called today. About two o'clock," Roger responded with a puzzled expression.

Lois looked at Roger with disapproval.

Roger, however, lucked out; it was not his fault this time. The hostess checked another sheet at the bottom of the pile and immediately gave the couple a bashful smile.

"Oh, yes. Here it is. I'm so sorry, sir. I just started my shift. Please follow me."

The hostess grabbed two menus and led the way. Lois held back a step, an accusatory expression still painted on her face.

"I thought you booked these yesterday," she pressed.

Roger was caught in a small, but real, lie. He preferred to think of it as a fib, the kind that husbands kept under their pillows. All he could do was smile and reply, "My little dynamite."

They walked up a small flight of carpeted stairs to the second level, where their table awaited. Lois admired the other couples. An elderly man and woman held hands while they waited for their meals. A woman about Lois' age at another table raised her fork to let her man sample her baked ziti. All Roger could think about was eating. The sight of food made him hungry and their long walk gave his eyes a feast.

"Is this okay?" the hostess asked.

"Yes, thank you," Roger replied as he held the chair for his wife. She smiled as she always did when he was so cordial.

"Your server will be right with you," the hostess confirmed as she gave each a menu before returning to her podium.

Roger and Lois took a moment to take in their new surroundings.

"This is nice. They changed the theme since we were here last time," Lois remarked.

"They had a glass theme before, right?" Roger observed.

Lois squinted her eyes in confusion. "I'm not sure. How come you remember things like that but you forget what's right in front of you?"

"Well, I don't know. I just have a lot on my plate right now."

"Your plate looks pretty empty to me right now." Lois gestured to the clean bread plate in front of him.

Roger didn't know why he remembered certain insignificant tidbits, some of which were downright odd. Both buried their heads in their menus. Lois immediately focused on the wine section. She loved the warm feeling of having a glass of wine and the immediate tipsiness she would feel, which only enhanced her lighthearted conversation with Roger. Before each had time to digest the menu's words, a burly twenty-five-year-old server gravitated toward their table.

"Hello there. My name is John and I will be your server. How are you two doing this evening?"

"We are fine, thanks," Roger said.

"Are you ready to order?" he asked.

The question caught both of them off guard. They barely had time to peruse the menu. Although they had eaten at the restaurant a few months back, the menu was updated extensively along with the theme. John noticed their hesitation and offered to return in a few minutes. Lois, however, was ready for her wine.

"How about some wine, Roger? Do you have a Lambrusco?"

Lois loved the sweet taste of a deep red Lambrusco. Although some said it tasted too much like simple grape juice, her taste buds always told her to order it.

"Yes we do. One or two glasses?" John responded with a smile.

Lois playfully nodded her head as she raised an eyebrow. She knew John was asking if he should bring two glasses, one for each of them, but she felt like playing with the two boys. Roger wasn't much of a drinker. Even in college, he only drank socially, but he didn't mind an occasional glass of wine. His answer was easy. Sharing the same drink with Lois made him feel closer to her for some reason.

"She could probably drink two at once, but I'll take the second. Thank you," Roger chuckled.

"Ha, I'll bring that right out," John replied.

Roger and Lois discussed the various dishes. This restaurant didn't discriminate. They offered the best from Mexico, Italy, France, and even a touch of Japan, which was something new since their last visit. Both were feeling Italian dishes. The next decision was to narrow down the choices. Roger persuaded Lois to go with the lasagna. She thought for a moment and accepted. She liked how Roger took charge when she was indecisive. If Lois was torn between the blue and the red dress at a department store, Roger's insight was usually the deciding factor. He chose to go with the spaghetti with meat sauce, something safe. He didn't want to ruin the night with a bad case of indigestion that he often received after experimenting with unknown foods.

"So, did you decide about our trip?" Lois asked.

"Actually, yes. I was thinking London. I mean Paris would be great, but we don't speak the language."

"But, what about the romance, the Louvre, the Eiffel Tower?" Lois retorted.

"London has romance. Hey, I'll be there. Romance is my middle name," Roger coyly responded.

"Romance is your middle name only on nights like this. *Work* is your real middle name. For our next trip, leave work at home. No more just bringing a book to read on the plane. Last time you were practically working from our hotel room." Lois remembered that last year when they went to the Caribbean, Roger had brought a briefcase along from the office. The simple case turned into a portable desk as he focused more on client portfolios than on snorkeling.

"Don't worry. I'll tell them I'm *really* on vacation this time," Roger stressed.

She grabbed Roger's hand and caressed it. Her touch was warm and soft, which consumed his focus and put his mind on nothing other than his cradled appendage. Lois had a twinkle in her eyes as she softly whispered, "Then maybe we can start working on that family of ours."

Lois' words made Roger perk up. He knew it was up to her when she wanted to start a family. After all, she had to carry the little tyke around for nine months. Before Roger could respond, John returned holding two tall glasses of red wine. He set one glass down in front of Lois, and then started to place the other glass in front of her. Both looked up at the brawny man and saw the smile on his face. He tried to add to the running joke from Lois' drink order, and it seemed to work. He slid the second glass in front of Roger and asked, "So, have we decided?"

"Yes. I believe we have. I'll have the spaghetti. And my beautiful wife will have the lasagna," Roger replied, taking charge. This put a smile on Lois' face.

"Good choices. Would you like the recommended sides with that?"

"Yes. That's fine."

John wrote on his notepad. "Will there be anything else?"

"Yes. There is one more thing," Roger replied.

He stood up, gravitated to his wife's side, and then held out his hand.

"What are you doing?" Lois asked.

"Just take my hand."

Lois placed her hand inside Roger's grasp, and then stood up. Her eyes squinted as she looked at John, who shrugged.

Roger reached into his pocket and removed the item he had carried with him from work, the item he had concealed inside his office desk, the item Lois had rested her eyes on last week during a stroll downtown.

"Open it," Roger said as he handed her the black case.

Lois did just that and beheld the necklace she had fallen in love with in that store window.

"You remembered!" Lois said.

"I'd never forget tonight."

Roger kissed his wife deeply. Then he whisked her hair aside and fastened the necklace.

John looked at them with eager eyes.

"Uh, did you need something else, sir?"

"I just wanted you to know that it's our anniversary."

"I'll make this a special night for you two." John smiled as he scurried on his way.

Roger and Lois sat quietly and basked in the shadowy, tranquil environment. Roger studied the diamond resting against Lois' radiating skin and the way it sparkled in her brown eyes. This moment was one that Roger cherished. When he would have a few minutes to himself after a busy meeting or a late-night business conference, he would close his eyes and transport himself to a moment like this.

Just as the couple enjoyed the silence together, a sudden outcry erupted from the entryway. Roger and Lois looked at the commotion, as did most of the guests around them.

A bum busted through the entryway door and lunged toward the hostess. She screamed in fright from the vagrant's unknown intentions. Without hesitation, the restaurant manager widened his eyes and hustled toward the intruder. He knew the occasional beggar would slip through the valet first line of defense and that these bums were more or less harmless, but their abrupt appearance was their involuntary downfall. The manager could not let this man disrupt the customers, *his* customers. The manager signaled to two muscular servers who sprang to action. Before the bum could cause any more disorder, the two servers ejected him out onto the concrete.

Roger shook his head from the actions. While he did feel sympathetic to some of the truly needy beggars, he wished these people would just get a job and leave the civilized folks to eat in peace. Perturbed, he looked at Lois and barked, "Geez. The nerve of these bums!"

4

The night air was cool and moist. Roger and Lois walked from their evening meal as she carried her leftover lasagna in a doggy bag. She hung onto her husband's arm as he gallantly led the way to the valet podium. Roger felt satisfied. The meal had hit the spot, and all he thought about was getting home to seduce his wife. Roger knew that Lois had one too many glasses of wine, but that was all right. He liked her when she was frisky, and it only added to his desire for her.

"I feel like we're on our first date," Lois gently whispered.

"I think someone had too much to drink...my little dynamite," Roger chuckled.

Lois watched Roger greet the valet driver with his claim ticket. The young man jumped to fetch the SUV as

Roger chatted with another valet driver about an exotic Porsche nearby. Lois liked to watch Roger interact with others. She liked how he stood tall and always knew how to direct the conversation. He was a man who lived in the moment and knew how to talk diplomatically. This was a skill, she figured, that must have been fostered from his years of working with big-time business clients.

Roger walked toward Lois, but as his eyes filled with his wife's glowing face, the roar of his SUV's gas-guzzling engine consumed his focus. It was followed by the sound of tires screeching. Roger flared up like a mother hearing a stranger abusing her child.

"Whoa! What the hell are you doing?" he shouted at the culprit.

The college-aged man had a look of embarrassment, as he realized that one of his customers had finally caught on to his joyriding. Roger helped Lois into the passenger's side, and then made his disapproval known to the other man.

"Come on. Where did you learn to drive? This is a fifty thousand dollar vehicle, not some beat-up wagon. And you just drive it around like you don't give a shit!" he blasted.

The valet driver gave no response. Roger stormed to the driver's side, purposely giving no tip.

It's about time someone stood up to these punks, he thought.

Lois could hear his scolding through the sound-deafening material of the SUV. She giggled, too tired to do anything, too tired even to click her seatbelt. All she wanted to do was bask. "Boys will be boys," she mouthed under her breath.

Roger grabbed the keys from the young man and entered the tranquility of his SUV. His nose received a hint of Lois' natural scent, which stimulated his receptive olfactory nerve. He immediately calmed down and put himself right back into the placid mood he had felt as he walked out.

"Let's go home and I'll make it all better," Lois murmured.

Her words massaged his auditory nerve and further pushed him into serenity. Roger glanced at his wife; her cleavage kneaded his optic nerve. His worries subsided.

Roger pulled out and drove down the familiar downtown streets. Lois' tipsiness heightened the mood and made him feel as if he were back in college driving home from an evening basketball game at the Bryce Jordan Center.

Lois began to sing. "Row, row, row your boat, gently down the stream—come on, Roger."

Roger laughed.

"Come on, sing," she playfully instructed.

Roger gave in and joined in the melody. He was a horrible singer, but having an intoxicated audience allowed even the worst singer to shine. They sang in tandem, Lois a few beats ahead of Roger, "…gently down the stream. Merrily, merrily, merrily, merrily, Life is but a dream…"

Lois moved closer to Roger and slid her hand on his thigh. Her libido was raging. The fun and games continued as Roger commanded the road. Then, like flipping a light switch, buckets of rainwater attacked his vehicle. Roger immediately reached for the wipers, but the rubber was no match for the flood of water mixed with golf-ball sized hail. He looked up at the sky. While it was relatively clear when they had left, ominous clouds now filled it, stealing the moon away.

Up head, Roger saw the Pleasant Place Bridge through the shield of water. He could make out the fact that four lanes existed, but the water made it nearly impossible to see where the other cars were.

Just follow the yellow line, he kept telling himself, remembering the driving manual he had studied as a teenager.

He couldn't make out what the body of water was doing down below, but he knew it must have been raging.

Lois continued the song in an attempt to keep up the light-hearted mood, but sweat covered Roger's brow. He hated driving in blinding weather, and although his SUV gave him a sense of protection, all he could think about was that yellow line.

Lois turned to look behind them, but as she did, she knocked the doggy bag from her lap onto the carpet.

"Watch the rug!" Roger instinctively yelled as he moved his eyes over to the lasagna spill.

As Roger removed his stare from the yellow line, he didn't see what fate brought the loving couple. Because the moment he looked back at the rain-covered road, he saw an image that would forever change his and his wife's life.

The image was two blinding headlights, but they weren't the headlights of a compact car, which would be the contender in a bout with Roger's champion SUV; they were the headlights of a monstrous, multi-ton tractor-trailer with a fully-weighted load. The truck was hungry as its trailer had jackknifed, which prevented an escape for its prey.

Roger looked up and had a split second of an aura, a moment where chaos met clarity. He could not think, or react, but just be in the moment. After time had bent, the tractor-trailer consumed Roger's SUV. Like a ragdoll, Lois flew forward and smashed through the front windshield, knocking her immediately unconscious. Her body ejected into the air and soared higher and higher over the concrete bridge. Just like an afflicted bird, however, Lois quickly plummeted toward the screaming water. Her body pierced through the liquid and entered the underwater world. The diamond necklace around her neck broke free and descended toward the unknown.

The tractor-trailer continued to devour more innocent victims on the bridge. A librarian on her way home from work and a soccer mom with her three children were no match for the menacing machine. Flames erupted and metal exploded, rendering the bridge into an impassable roadblock. Cars swerved and nailed the embankment as their drivers took the lesser of two evils. As turmoil blasted everywhere, the truck finally ground to a halt, sending flames of ignited diesel fuel hundreds of feet into the air. Rain blanketed the area, but the fires were too intense even for the liquid from above.

Two bystanders in the oncoming lane had the most horrific view of the show, as they watched the hungry machine eat its victims. What mesmerized them in particular was Lois' swan dive into the unknown below. Both slammed on their brakes and hustled toward the location of Lois' descent.

"A woman! I think a woman's in the water!" one of the two bystanders screamed.

The other bystander, a swimming coach named Bill, didn't say a word, because he knew that words wouldn't, they couldn't, save the fallen woman. Bill dove off the twenty-foot high structure without hesitation. As he soared through the air, he knew the dive was dangerous even for a seasoned high diver, but as his face smashed into the harsh water, adrenaline quickly pushed his fears away.

A crowd watched from the bridge. All they could see was the bobbing water with no sign of Lois or her savior. Seconds seemed liked minutes as the crowd's eyes tried to search for any sign of life. Some pondered diving in themselves, but they had to give the diver a few more seconds to succeed.

Finally, after what seemed like infinity, Bill emerged from the raging water different from the way he had entered; he had Lois on his back. Bill gasped for oxygen before he embarked on the hundred-yard swim to the south shore. Although a hundred yards would be a brisk morning workout for the veteran swimmer, he knew this would be the most important one hundred yards of not only his life, but also the life of the stranger on his back.

Meanwhile, on the chaotic bridge, Roger still sat inside his SUV. But the moment his head had bashed into the leather-wrapped steering wheel, his mind left his body. Roger was off in a distant universe, a place where even dreams failed to exist. And if he were given the choice, he would have chosen to be somewhere without thoughts rather than pinned inside his demolished vehicle. As blood trickled down his cut face, his motionless mug lay against the deflated airbag. If he had been somehow awake, the picture of him and Lois, inches from his eyes, would have filled his gaze, but the photograph would have been very different from the one he remembered. It was split down the middle, separating him from his wife.

Fortunately for Roger, more members of the crowd assessed the destroyed vehicles on the bridge. Brazen men, who naturally assumed the responsibility of hero during times of despair, had stepped up during the minutes it took for rescue workers to reach the chaos. Two brothers, who were driving together several cars behind Roger, took notice of his SUV. They ran to his side as the sound of the blaring ambulance sirens grew in strength.

"Sir, can you hear me!?" yelled the older of the brothers.

Roger failed to respond, but that didn't stop the two men.

"We've got to get him out!" the younger brother yelled.

Both men went to work on Roger, grabbing and pulling at his outwardly lifeless body. As they exerted their strength, the rear of the SUV ignited into flames, which traveled under the vehicle toward the twenty-six gallon fuel tank.

"His belt! His seatbelt is still on!" roared the older brother.

Both knew that at any moment the SUV could consume them. However, that didn't stop their drive, as they knew exactly what had to be done. Both brothers worked in tandem as the elder reached around and pressed the seatbelt release. Miraculously, it still functioned as the click of the metal clasp resonated inside the smashed cabin, bringing music to the brothers' ears. The older brother unlatched the belt, while the younger gave the first yank. Roger's body slid out like a baby from a birth canal. Both men focused on moving as far away as possible.

They dragged Roger fifteen feet, and then, in a sudden flash—boom! The vehicle exploded into a fireball of fury. At the same moment, an ambulance driving from the north side took wind of the brothers' action. The ambulance screeched to a stop nearby as two paramedics burst from the back.

"Is he alright!?" the skinny paramedic yelled.

"I don't know. We pulled him from that SUV," replied the older brother as they all glanced at the burning remains of Roger's SUV.

The other paramedic, the seasoned veteran, checked Roger for signs of life. He positioned his finger on his neck, felt something, but was not sure if the thump was a heartbeat or the vibration of the unstable bridge. He repositioned his finger.

"I have a pulse!" he finally blurted.

"We've got to get him to Saint Peters North Hospital," his colleague shouted.

With perfect timing, the driver of the ambulance, a hefty paramedic, ran toward Roger's body with a gurney. His job was to drive, something he deeply enjoyed for more than twenty years. But more importantly, he was the strength of the trio—the polished pistons in a well-tuned engine.

At the south-end of the bridge, bystanders feverishly helped the injured as more ambulances raced to the scene. Off on the side, Bill the swimmer finally reached the shore. He was breathing vigorously as his lungs tried to compensate for the extra hundred pounds of nearly dead weight. He finally made it, rolling Lois onto the muddy shore. Luckily, for Bill, he was not alone as a fellow Good Samaritan, an off-duty fireman, followed his breast-stroke from the bridge above. As the fireman neared the rocky path down to the shoreline, he saw a blaring ambulance racing toward him.

"Over here! Hey, over here!" the fireman screamed as he flailed his arms.

The ambulance slammed on its brakes near the pathway down to the beach.

"Hey! Down here!" Bill yelled from his spot as the fireman with a brother-sister team of paramedics hustled toward him.

"She's in bad shape. She flew off the bridge. I don't know which car she was in. Oh God, it's a mess up there," Bill explained to the three wide-eyed individuals.

"Let's get her up the hill," the female paramedic instructed.

Bill was exhausted, and her words seemed to travel right to his overexerted muscles. Fortunately, the random bystander helping was a brawny fireman, who had a fresh set of biceps to aid in hauling Lois' debilitated body.

They carried her to the top of the hill as Bill took notice of her right arm bobbling like a spraying fire hose. It was fractured—at the least. The contorting arm made him cringe. As they reached the top, the driver, an aged paramedic, awaited with medical gear and a gurney. They placed her on top of the bed, which the rain had soaked, and then began to work on her. Lois' wet neck gave the female paramedic trouble as she searched for a sign of a beating heart. As the crowd waited without speech, and without thought, the female paramedic finally spoke.

"I feel a faint pulse!" she exclaimed.

The older paramedic positioned a suctioning device on Lois's mouth and began to squeeze in and out, attempting to pull out the water sloshing around inside her lungs. He worked vigorously, as he knew the right amount of pressure and positioning that would expel the water. Suddenly, water oozed from Lois' mouth. Her breathing resumed, albeit faint and muffled.

"That's a good sign, but I don't know if she's going to make it," explained the brother paramedic.

His sister looked at the two men covered in mud from their climb up the hill. "Are you guys okay?"

"Yeah, I'll be alright," the fireman responded.

Bill was physically and mentally exhausted. He wanted to explain how he had taken a swan dive face first off the bridge, and then swam a hundred yards carrying the woman. He didn't, and simply replied, "I'll live."

The aged paramedic looked at the wreckage on the bridge blocking traffic and realized that traveling through the air or water was their only option. He yelled to his colleagues, "The bridge is impassable! It's a drive, but we've got to get her to Southern General Hospital!"

"More help is on the way. Thank you, guys," the female paramedic said to the two saviors.

They watched as the paramedics positioned Lois' unconscious body into the back of the ambulance. Her sexy dress was torn and a mixture of mud and blood covered her once radiating skin. The older paramedic jumped into the driver's seat and punched the gas pedal. He pointed the vehicle's nose back the way it had come.

Police cars, motorists, and ambulances flurried around the war zone on both sides of the burning wreckage. Nothing or no one was protected from the all-encroaching rain, which seemed to intensify with the lights and sirens. There was no way for anyone to use the bridge as it was intended, to cross the raging body of water. Since the only other detour was a fifteen mile drive east to the other bridge, the ambulances were forced to return to one of the city's two major hospitals—one in the north-end, the other in the south-end. While the turmoil-filled area bustled with activity, two of these ambulances raced at similar speeds, were commanded by similarly experienced drivers, and held a respective member of the Belkin family. The major difference between these two speeding vehicles, however, was not that they held different unconscious occupants; it was the fact they traveled in opposite directions, moving farther and farther apart with each passing second. Just as the scorched photograph inside the remains of Roger's SUV was torn down the middle, separating the couple, both now faced a much greater separation.

5

The sound of a heartbeat monitor filled the softly lit hospital room at Saint Peters North Hospital. The beats were slow and rhythmic and filled sixty seconds with precisely fifty-eight. Roger lay motionless on the soft bed, dressed only in a blue gown. Sensors were plugged into his body and a heavy bandage was wrapped tightly around his head. He entered the modern hospital exactly thirty-two minutes after the moment of impact and was treated by some of the city's top emergency room doctors. Saint Peters North was the most modern hospital in the city and was tall and wide enough to provide most patients with a private room—a fact that led many individuals to request the state-of-the-art facility for a hospital stay. Of course, Roger didn't have a choice; he was brought to Saint Peters North because it was the only option from the impassable bridge.

At nearly four p.m. the next day, like clockwork, two nurses entered to check on Roger's condition. Melissa was new to the hospital. She was shadowing Judy, a twenty-three year veteran of the nursing profession.

"How's he doing?" Melissa asked.

Judy checked his bandaged head. "His head will be hurting for a while. He's lucky he made it. A father and son in a car out there didn't even have a chance last night."

Melissa raised her hand to her mouth at the mere thought of the chaotic bridge. Although she loved to help those in need, she hated to think about the pain and suffering others faced.

"Oh dear, how many total?" Melissa asked.

"So far, three dead and nine injured. Everything is just so hectic."

"I can't believe what happened. It seems what could go wrong, went wrong," Melissa said softly as she took a deep breath. "Do we have all nine here?"

"No, we have five here. Southern General has four," Judy explained.

Both leaned in to Roger and watched his chest rise with each involuntary breath. Melissa wondered whether this handsome man had a family. If he did, where were they?

Southern General Hospital, the historically older hospital in the city, housed a similar room with dim lights and hospital machines. This room, however, had even more critical devices plugged into the room's occupant, Lois Belkin. Lois arrived forty-six minutes after the moment of impact as Southern General was across the city. She was covered in a blue gown and had a look of exhaustion on her face. Lois had more trouble with the E.R. team last night, as unconsciousness triggered her body to surrender to a comatose state.

Lois was fortunate to be staying at Southern General, not because of having a private room or high-tech equipment, but due to the full-time head nurse on the recovery floor. Nurse Ann Stevens was a nurse's nurse, with her mothering and nurturing approach to health care and recovery. She firmly believed that it was just as important to talk to patients and offer them compassion whether they were awake or dormant. Although she was only thirty-seven, she had received the hospital alliance's "Nurse of the Year" award six times in the past fifteen-years.

As Lois lay on the undemanding bed, mind separated from body, her heartbeats echoed off the stark white walls. The low-angled sun outlined the drawn blinds, which meant a stop by the floor nurse. Normally, one of Nurse Ann's runners would do the honors, but she quickly took Lois under her wing after her late-night arrival. This was not because others on her floor were less important, but because no one knew Lois' name. She was referred to as "Jane Doe" upon arrival, and Nurse Ann wanted to uncover the identity of the fallen angel left on her doorstep.

Nurse Ann led the new shift doctor into Lois' lair as the gray-haired man checked his chart.

"…and this one was rescued out of the water. Do we have any identification?" the doctor asked.

"No, doctor. No pockets on the dress she was wearing," Nurse Ann replied.

"Her chart says she has an arm fracture and had some internal bleeding, but it looks like the E.R. stabilized her last night. I hope she pulls out of the coma. There really is very little we can do now but wait," added the doctor, who checked the sleeping woman listed as "Jane Doe" in his chart.

"The police were here earlier. I think they're going to try to track down her identity," Nurse Ann responded.

She leaned in close and placed her hand on Lois' cheek, her radiating skin now pale and colorless. Lois' face felt cold and lifeless to Nurse Ann as she combed the sleeping woman's eyebrow with her fingertip. Then, she moved closer, positioned her mouth near Lois' ear, and whispered softly like a warm morning breeze, "Who are you, dear? I'm sure someone out there misses you."

6

The sun was setting outside Roger's hospital window. The light lowered in his room, bringing it closer to darkness. His heartbeat monitor seemed to pick up beats. Then, Roger's arm twitched ever so slightly as the beats escalated. The spasm went to his left leg, and then to his right. Roger opened his eyes. A sudden burst of images filled his mind. His black SUV, rainwater, his large office, and, most predominately, Lois in a black dress all spun around and tingled his brain's neurons. Then, like a light bulb popping, all of the images vanished from his mind. Roger focused on the situation at hand and sat up. He looked around the hospital room with a baffled expression.

What the hell happened?

With his mind's little voice asking that simple question, he immediately felt throbbing pain overwhelm his head. Roger touched the thick gauze tightly wrapping his forehead. He let out a bellow. His attention shifted to his ear, filled with the rapid sound of an electronic heartbeat, *his* heartbeat. Roger found himself in the worst place he could possibly awaken. He had never actually stayed in a hospital overnight except for one time as a seven-year-old child after undergoing a frightening tonsillectomy. However, his mother fought the staff and stayed by his side throughout his stay, calming him. That could be why he had felt such animosity toward doctors and hospitals, but whatever the reason, he wanted to get as far away from his location as possible. He wished he had awoken in his cushy bed, or in a hotel room on a business trip, or even at his office, as sometimes he took a ten minute catnap during his lunch hour. Unfortunately, he wasn't in any of these locations. His mahogany desk and beta fish in clear water were actually a metallic bed with bars and a catheter filled with yellow urine. In addition, the man normally dressed in a costly Hugo Boss suit with a tailored shirt was now covered in a two-dollar blue gown resistant to vomit and other bodily fluids.

As Roger scanned the room trying to make sense of his dilemma, he suddenly felt abandoned. He wondered how he had ended up inside this prison cell. Most importantly, where was the love of his life? One thing was perfectly clear to him; he had to remove himself from his surroundings. Roger knew his mind would not be free until he returned to a familiar environment, where he could try to lift the low hanging cloud obscuring his mind.

Roger looked for any sign of life. The only communication he found within immediate reach was a phone on the end table. Roger picked it up, balancing IV lines with phone cords, and began dialing home.

"Four...Five...No, no, Two..." Roger mouthed as he pressed each digit.

The businessman realized his phone number was lost from his mind, corrupted like a computer's hard drive after a deadening shock.

"Hello? Hello? Who's there?" a baritone voice expelled through the phone as Roger's mind screamed.

Roger tried to hang up the phone, but it fell, smashing on the ground. He mouthed the word "Lois," as his whisper seemed to travel beyond the thick walls. He hoped it would reach the woman he had so desperately craved. As the seconds passed, he realized the stark truth that the biggest bout of forgetfulness of his entire life faced him. His only crutch was years of higher education to aid his reasoning. The first step in tackling any colossal problem, he concluded, was to deal with the immediate situation at hand.

The heartbeat monitor focused his attention, which led to the realization that a plethora of electronic sensors had been artificially attached to his body. Without thought, he pulled the various wires from his wrist and hand. He could feel the narrow tube of the intravenous slide out from the engorged vein in his hand, which made him wince. Through the sting, he grabbed the many sensors taped to his chest and abdomen and ripped them from his body, taking some hair with them. The heart monitor changed to a flat, stabbing beep that filled the room, and his head, with the sound of death. Quickly, he swung his feet around and dangled them off the bed, but something felt odd. He had a feeling in his groin that he had never felt before. It was as if something was unnaturally poking deep within his abdomen and, with each movement on the bed, it dug farther into him. Roger flipped up the blue gown and saw a long tube coiling around his leg. He followed it up, and what he saw shocked him; the tube did not end on the outside of his body, it traveled into the urethra of his penis. Roger squeezed the tube and pulled slightly, and with each movement, he could feel it poking deep within his body. His breathing escalated and sweat drenched his face. The image of the catheter burned into his mind, and he was beginning to hyperventilate. Roger knew he had to pull it out quickly, or he would fall back into the unknown void.

Just like a bandage, he thought.

Roger turned his head and reached down to his groin; he firmly gripped the tube and yanked. He felt the hose pull out from his body followed by a burst of fluid. Roger was terrified to look down, afraid to see gushing red blood spewing from his delicate penis. He barely mustered the strength and saw the yellow color of urine dribble from the uncorked apparatus.

Roger took a moment and focused on the closed door in front of him. He looked at the light from the hallway casting through the door's window and tried to forget the unsettling images of his catheter removal. He hoped these pictures would be purged from his mind's database and never retrieved again.

Roger planted his feet on the cold, hard tile, which made his mind refocus on the nerves on his soles, temporarily taking the pain away from his upper body. He stood up and shuffled to the door like a toddler taking his first steps. Roger finally stopped to glance through the window of his cell into the brightly lit hallway. Roger opened the door and glanced left, and then right. He saw medical equipment lining the hallway with banks of identical doorways. The thought of Lois suddenly entered his mind. He pondered her existence sleeping in one of the adjacent hospital rooms. Roger used his strength to move toward the next room. Inside was an obese creature Roger assumed was male; however, he couldn't be sure as thick gauze wrapped the person's entire body, including the head. Roger lurched toward another door. He peered inside, as a wrinkly male patient lunged at him from the shadows. Roger wobbled on his feet from the surprise, and then toppled over to the unyielding floor; his head bashed the wall sending a flood of pain to his skull. The elderly man slammed the door and retreated inside his room, bringing the hallway back to silence. Roger's bizarre environment made him crave his home even more. He rubbed his head, and then picked himself up, but pain shot down his right leg.

The lost businessman tottered down the hallway. His gown had a slit open in the back as cool air grazed his backside. Suddenly, Roger heard two approaching voices—one voice was deep and resolute, and the other was somewhat higher, but still masculine.

"I'm looking for Lois Belkin. Where is she?" Roger asked the two approaching male nurses.

Both men neared the lost patient with wide eyes and wide grasps.

"You have to go back to your room," the taller nurse said.

"Where is Lois?" Roger continued.

"There is no Lois here. Let's get you back to your room," the shorter one said as he gripped Roger's arm.

"Hey! Let me go," Roger snapped.

"We're just trying to help. Your head is not right. You need to rest," the taller nurse insisted.

Roger panicked from the grip of the four claws. He gave in.

"Now, where is your room?" the taller nurse asked.

Roger nodded down the hall behind him. The three of them moved toward the wrong direction. Roger felt scared, alone, lost. He had to escape.

A crowd of visitors swarmed them. Roger saw an opening. He used all of his energy to break free. Roger ducked between two women, and then fled down the hallway.

"Hey! Stop! Get back here!" the taller nurse yelled.

Roger was free. He ran through the pain, turned down a hallway, and then hid inside a room. He wanted nothing more than to go home, to go to a safe place to solve the questions that hung over him. But Roger realized that just like his phone number, the phone number to safety, he didn't even remember his address.

Roger watched from inside the room as the men passed. The threat was averted. As he turned to exit the room, a strange man startled him. Roger recognized that the man resembled himself, but he had cuts and bruises on his grubby face and wore a tight bandage around his head. Then, Roger realized the man was actually reflecting back from a mirror; he was seeing the image of himself.

"What happened to you?" he asked the stranger staring at him.

Roger looked deep into the man's hazel eyes. He longed to find the lost memory that held his home address. His mind throbbed with pain, but Roger kept trying, kept focusing. And then like a ray of light penetrating a black cloud, Roger blinked.

"Dietrich Road," he whispered.

Roger grabbed a pen from a table nearby and scribbled the two words on his wrist. He tried to remember the street number, but numbers appeared to be the most damaged in his mind.

With an ounce of hope, Roger looked around the dark room and noticed a figure lying in the bed. He sneaked around the curtain and saw an elderly man asleep and unaware of the intrusion. Roger looked down at the blue gown covering his aching body, and then shifted his eyes to a pile of perfectly folded clothes on a chair nearby. The simple sight made him suddenly strive for Lois. She sometimes laid out an outfit for him in the morning on a chair if he was running late and in the shower. He wished it were one of those mornings.

Roger began to disrobe the blue gown and felt the cool air against his naked body. It felt purifying and tickled his sensitive skin. He took a second to glance down at his exposed penis, which was his cue to dress rapidly. Roger grabbed the dark-colored pants and slid them on his legs through the pain. He noticed his right leg involuntarily twitched as he raised it, and concluded it must have been a result of his affliction. He grabbed the light-colored dress shirt and began to button it up, as he did every morning before work. Roger finished and instinctively tucked the shirt into the pants, giving a sense of neatness to the outfit. He slid into a pair of loafers that were under the chair. Luckily, the shoes were a perfect fit. Roger took a step into the brighter light cast from the hallway, and then stopped cold. His attention focused on the pants, which were riding up several inches to his ankles. Roger peered at the man lying horizontally in the bed and tried to assess his height. Even though Roger was a few inches taller than average, those inches rested in his torso. He noticed a photograph propped on the bedside table. It showed the elderly man wearing a vivacious smile as he gripped a similarly aged woman close to his side. The couple looked happy and peaceful, enjoying a moment together that would forever be captured in the snapshot. Roger looked at the man's now bewildered face, which was pale and unresponsive.

What happened? Roger thought. He realized his intention in looking at the photograph was to find out the man's height. He noticed the man was comically shorter than the woman; he reasoned that either she was unnaturally tall or he was unusually short. Roger looked down at the high-water pants and knew the latter was the hand to bet.

The stranger in the mirror stopped Roger again, as he took a moment to fix his shirt. Roger performed an unconscious polish to his collar whenever he saw a mirror, an instinct ingrained in him from years in the business world. Roger studied his weary face as he grabbed the head bandage and threw it aside. He knew it had to go, as it was a sure sign of his jailbreak. With the problem of appearance mostly solved, Roger was ready to embark on the next stage of his journey.

7

Roger stepped into the lit hallway of Saint Peters North Hospital. The pain in his right leg intensified as he tried to walk it off. Roger hoped his new attire would be enough to convince any potential barricades, particularly a hospital staff member. Up ahead, a bank of closed elevators lined the hallway as Roger took a moment to check the area. He knew this would be the ideal place for parked individuals and the prime opportunity for small talk, his current worst enemy. Fortunately, he saw nothing and no one, just up and down arrows offering a choice to the elevator's future patrons. Roger pressed the down arrow and waited. He wished they had made another button, one that would provide a private elevator for those individuals not interested in chatting with a random stranger.

Why do people always have to talk? Why can't they just stand in silence? he mused. Roger realized this was just the way humans reacted, craving some meaningless prattle to pass the typical thirty-seconds of silence.

What was a person's fear? he pondered. He reasoned people feared offending others by remaining silent. Roger was hoping that no one would be on the elevator, as he had no brainpower to think of a clever excuse for his visit to this floor.

A ding emitted and the down arrow illuminated. Roger licked his lips as he waited for the doors to open. The doors spread and, to Roger's dismay, a middle-aged man stood inside the confined space. Roger hoped this man would be on a cell phone or engrossed in a newspaper, but the moment the doors opened, his eyes locked with Roger's and he appeared eager for the new occupant to join him on his descent.

Roger stepped on and saw the button marked "G" glowing. He took a step back so that he was behind the stranger, hoping this distance would discourage any direct queries.

The doors shut, and then silence consumed the two men. No trite music or voice-over announcement resonated, just the loudness of silence.

The man took a step to his side, and then looked over at Roger's beaten face and messy hair, moving down to his short pants.

"Man, you look like you just got hit by a truck," the man chuckled. "Hey, where's the flood?" he added with a bigger laugh.

Roger kept his eyes straight, completely ignoring the man.

Maybe he will get the idea that I don't want to talk, he hoped.

The ding of the bottom floor saved Roger, drawing his eyes up to the illuminated "G." The doors opened to a floor much like the one Roger had left, save for the flurry of people lining the hall.

The man maintained eye contact with Roger, curious about his lack of response. Roger scurried into the ground floor.

"Hey, buddy. Are you alright?" the man yelled, as he realized Roger might have been in distress.

Roger focused all of his attention on running from the stranger. He moved into the hall as a hint of relief filled his mind. With his attention focused on departing the elevator, he did not see two male paramedics lurking nearby.

"Hey! Watch out!" yelled one of the men from the collision.

Roger's fear of apprehension overwhelmed him as the two paramedics stopped and looked scornfully at him. Roger stumbled, not looking back. He hoped he would not feel a tug on his shoulder from one of the hospital "wardens."

Roger scampered through the dense crowd, weaving between passing bodies like a stalked deer using oak trees as cover. He hoped his path would lead to an exit of the prison, but he realized he didn't know his exact location. While he did visit Southern General Hospital a few times when his boss had been in for heart bypass surgery, this didn't look like Southern General. He convinced himself that once outside, things should become clearer on how to get home.

Finally, Roger came to a crossroads. He saw two signs pointing down two different hallways, one toward the "Front Parking Lot," the other to the "Rear Parking Lot." Roger pondered the choice.

The front would probably be easier to figure out my location. Maybe my car is parked outside with Lois waiting to pick me up?

He realized, however, that things were probably much more complicated. Roger decided to take the "front" hallway, but just as he began to walk, he saw several police officers heading his way. He wondered if they were on to his escape and were looking for individuals who matched Roger's description. Whatever their intention, his choice changed to the "rear" hallway.

Roger hustled down his chosen path. Then, like seeing the ribbon at a marathon's finishing line, the doorway to the free world revealed itself. He picked up his steps and blindsided a passing nurse. Roger didn't care, for he could smell the sweet scent of safety.

As Roger emerged, rays of the setting sun warmed his pale face. He basked in the openness. Roger let his eyes adjust to the natural light as he focused his ears on the sound of distant birds chirping. He felt like a free man, just released from an undeserving prison sentence. As he enjoyed his new freedom, the throbbing pain in his head returned, this time even worse. Then, his right leg locked. It was as if the plug that energized his ailing body had been ripped from its socket. He thought that maybe it was the artificial drugs that had once pumped into his veins, but now were abandoned in his hospital cell like everything else. Whatever the cause, his mind felt overwhelmed as mounting questions clouded his judgment.

"I've got to get home," he convinced himself. He would do whatever it took to get as far away from the hospital as possible.

Roger staggered through the packed parking lot. All of the cars started to blend, white SUVs looked black, and compacts appeared as full-sized. He hoped he would find his parked SUV, the mighty machine. He felt safe inside that vehicle and wanted so badly to grip its leather-wrapped steering wheel. Roger made it to the end of the lot and had no idea what to do. He turned to take in the soaring building mocking him, which only strengthened his desire to flee. As his senses shrieked, Roger saw two cars nearby. One was a beat-up sedan that was idling, its exhaust pipes spewing murky, oil-burnt smoke. A junky truck was parked next to it. Two men used the rusty vehicle for support as they conversed. One was a rough looking African-American; the other was a stocky Hispanic man with a shaved head. Roger watched as the men cackled and seemed to forget about the idling sedan. He picked up bits of their conversation, which focused on the bizarre downpours the city had experienced over the past few days.

Without hesitation, Roger moved toward the deserted car. Normally, committing a crime would be the last thing he would ever consider, but he didn't care about some street-tough's junker. He had to take matters into his own hands. His only care in the world was trying to get to Lois. He needed her, and he knew she needed him, wherever she was.

"Hey, asshole. Can I help you?" snarled the husky Hispanic man as Roger let himself into the running car.

The man was baffled. He hesitated, as he expected a baggy-clothed hoodlum to be a carjacker, but the man he was watching, one dressed in business clothes with high pants, was not the stereotypical thief. The Hispanic man's mind quickly refocused on his vehicle as he saw Roger firmly planted in the driver's seat. He ran to the half-open window and reached for Roger.

"Hey! Whoa! Whoa! What are you doing?" he screamed, but Roger slammed the car into drive and nailed the gas.

The roaring engine mocked the enraged man as a cloud of black smoke covered him.

"I don't believe this!" the man yelled as he watched his car speed away.

It was nearly dark as Roger raced down the urban road trying to navigate the clumsy vehicle. His driving resembled an alcoholic heading home from a bar after a hard day's work. Roger's drug, however, was not alcohol; it was a mixture of pain, rage, and bewilderment. Cars zipped by, people walked, as the clunker squealed with each turn. Roger kept the gas floored and focused on balancing the car down the road, something he never had to do with his stout and perfectly engineered SUV. The car had horrible body sway, reacting to a turn like a soapbox car with skateboard-sized wheels.

Roger glanced at his wrist, but the scribbled street address only taunted him. A shopping district came into view with grocery stores and fast-food restaurants. Roger scanned the area. A horn suddenly blared. Two headlights blinded him. Roger refocused his drifting attention.

Up ahead, a small ice cream shop stood under the darkening sky. The sign out front in bright lights read "Scoopers." A group of kids burst from a soccer mom's mini-van as Roger widened his eyes.

"I know this place," he mumbled.

It was his favorite dessert spot. The rear of the business had an eighteen-hole miniature golf course, and he and Lois would frequently enjoy a Saturday evening game of golf in the summer. After Lois' usual win, both indulged in their favorite treat—two scoops of chocolate chip cookie dough in a dish.

Our house is close.

Roger wished he was driving back home on one of those summer nights with Lois by his side. He smiled as the memories flourished in his mind, and then he glanced to the right. Instead of seeing the image of Lois in colorful capris and a blouse, he saw duct tape covering the puke-green vinyl seat. Roger gripped the wheel tighter and said, "I'll be home soon."

8

The Belkin house sat under the freshly dark sky. The lights in most of the surrounding homes shined brightly through their drawn curtains. The suburban neighborhood was peaceful around this time as kids were off the streets doing their homework or playing video games, and those that were going out for the evening had already left.

Like a gust of wind, the roar of a muffler-less vehicle pierced the tranquility. Its misaimed headlights pointed toward the Belkin home. Inside, a grin covered Roger's face, as he maneuvered the tired horse toward his castle. The familiar landmarks reminded him of a return trip home from a long day's work. He was always eager to get home to see his wife, who took the stressors of the world away. This particular trip was his most anticipated. It didn't matter that he had no idea why he woke up half-dead, or without any clothes, or, most importantly, without Lois. He hoped that all of his questions would be answered when he pulled into his driveway.

Finally, Roger saw his towering house sitting as he always remembered it. He was glad to see something familiar, an environment in which he felt safe. The driveway was bare and all of the lights were off.

No SUV, he thought.

Roger aimed for the driveway, but the vehicle didn't respond as he expected. He popped the curb and the shoddy brakes left the car halfway on the lawn. The noise was probably enough to wake the whole street, but all he thought was, *Thank God I'm home.*

Roger used his shoulder to open the stubborn door. The force caused him to spill to the ground. He took a moment to collect himself, as his aching muscles overwhelmed his focus.

The front door stood closed in darkness as Roger stumbled toward it. Even though the lights were out, he hoped that Lois would whisk open the door and bring him in to clean his wounds. However, she did not appear. Roger realized he had to go in alone. He gave the doorknob a twist, but it was locked. He suddenly felt trapped, locked out of his own home and his old life. A weird out-of-body feeling came over him as he felt as if he were an imposter. He thought that maybe the real Roger was inside, and he would soon open the door to bark at this masquerading bum.

Roger suddenly remembered the fail-safe key he and Lois had hidden, but the exact details were tough for him to recall. Things like this were the first deleted from his memory, or at least misplaced. He glanced at the shrubbery, and then to some ornaments propped by the door. Nothing looked like a viable hiding spot, except for three stout flowerpots on the ground. Roger moved one aside, saw nothing useful, and then pushed the second. A small object appeared that resembled a key, but as soon as it began squirming, Roger knew it was a worm unhappy about the disturbance. Finally, he maneuvered the third pot, and a shiny silver key greeted him.

"There it is," he mumbled.

Roger bent down, but quickly winced from a sharp pain that flowed through his back. He took a deep breath and grabbed the key. Then, he slid it into the lock, opening the door to the castle.

A subtle smell attached to a soft breeze invigorated Roger's senses. It was hard to describe in words, like trying to explain the taste of water, but it was the scent of something familiar, something safe. Roger stared into the dark entryway. The moonlight cast a silhouette around Roger's aching frame. After a moment, he flipped on a light.

"Lois?" Roger said as his voice echoed in the sizable structure. All he received, however, was the sound of silence, the last sound he wanted to hear.

Where can she be? What happened?

More questions filled his clouded mind, and the last thing he wanted to do was think. Roger moved toward the kitchen as he stopped at the room's doorway. Before hitting the lights, he took in the darkness, absorbing the mystery that the absence of light had created. He could see his frame cast in front of him, outlined by the sole light shining from the bright entryway behind.

Roger turned on the light and perused the open kitchen. The floral arrangement sat perfectly on the table, still blooming from yesterday's picking. Clean dishes lay on a drain board near the sink and a basket on the counter still contained ripe fruit. All of these signs meant something to a skilled detective, but they only confused the exhausted Roger.

"Everything looks normal," he said, but the one thing missing from this perfect environment was Lois.

Roger made the rounds in the kitchen when something caught his eye. The liquor cabinet, storing some of the family's most precious jewels, seemed to have a radiating glow. He heeded the sign and gravitated toward it.

Roger finally took a sigh of relief, even though it would be short lived and artificial. He slid open the cabinet and checked the bottles of liquor. He wasn't a man who lived by the bottle, but a drink in the evening was welcomed after a rough day. Based on his calculation, he would need the whole cabinet, and then some, to compensate for his debilitating day. He pushed aside some rum, and moved a large jug of unopened Lambrusco to the top of the cabinet. Roger studied the wine for a moment, as he knew it was Lois' favorite. Finally, he grabbed the strong stuff in the back, a bottle of "Jack Daniel's Old Tennessee Whiskey." He struggled with the sealed cap like an old man with arthritis. Finally, he put the opened bottle to his cracked lips, and then took a long drink, each gulp rhythmically tuned.

"Ahhh," he exhaled.

He ventured upstairs, the clump of his footsteps filling the house as he floundered up each step. The hallway was dark. Roger used his damaged memory to guide him to his bedroom. He flipped the lights on as the master bedroom greeted him. The perfectly made queen-sized bed sat in the middle with his dresser and nightstand all in order. Everything was just as the couple had left it from their date just twenty-four hours ago. But all Roger could think about was finding something that solved the conundrum—a note, a message, or…Lois.

Roger took another swig of liquor, and then placed the bottle on the dresser. He moved to the attached bathroom. He looked at a towel hanging over the shower door. Lois would usually take it down before bed and toss it into the clothesbasket, but the fact that it still hung in its place suggested Lois' absence since last night.

Where is Lois? he thought.

On the counter stood a small tube of lipstick with a deep shade of red painting the top of the case. It focused his attention like a diamond teasing a thief. As Roger moved toward the object, his eyes refocused on the stranger reflecting back from the bathroom mirror. The man resembled Roger, but had ratty hair, bruises marring his skin, and a look of anguish in his eyes. Suddenly, a picture flashed into Roger's mind of him standing at the mirror, mesmerized by his reflection. The image, however, was not of this stranger; it was of the robust body of the real Roger. Suddenly, he felt a chill run through his body. His movements stopped, and so did his breathing. Roger was lost inside his mind trying to clutch the memories buried deep within the bowels of his brain. Then in a flash, he returned, gasping for air.

"What the hell happened to you?" he mouthed.

Roger went back into the bedroom. He grabbed the whiskey and downed another gulp, trying to speed up the alcoholic escape induced by the seedy substance. A picture caught his eye on the nightstand near the bed. He picked it up and studied the image of him with Lois embracing in a park under the sunny summer sky. This was a memory he remembered; it was from last summer after a bike ride through the city park. Lois bought Roger a digital camera, and he brought it on their day trip through the outdoors. A resting jogger stopped and offered his service as an impromptu cameraman to capture the couple together. Roger outlined Lois' body with his blackened fingertip, wishing the glossy paper was actually her supple skin. As his wife consumed his senses, he felt a tingle deep within his brain. The tingle quickly led to a throbbing sting that caused his eyes to flutter and to lose focus. The room began to spin like a drunken ride on the

Tilt-A-Whirl. Roger steered for his bed, but in a sudden burst, he saw black.

The battered businessman awoke in a park sitting on a blanket. He focused his eyes and saw a serene lake in the distance.

Where am I? he pondered.

The sun felt warm against his skin and the air smelled fresh, but Roger felt like a puppet. He tried to speak but couldn't. He tried to move, but his muscles were unresponsive; they were as if controlled by someone else. His mind still worked, however, and it made him wonder whether he was, in fact, dead. Whatever the situation, he could see through this man's eyes, which received the breathtaking image of Lois drinking a glass of wine. A soft breeze blew, sweeping her autumn brown hair from her face. Lois raised the wine glass, swirling the red liquid. She smiled.

In a flash, the image of a swanky restaurant filtered into Roger's mind. Again, he felt paralyzed, seeing through a counterpart's eyes. Lois was wearing a dark dress with spaghetti straps draping around her shoulders. A burly server brought two plates of food, lasagna for Lois and a plate of spaghetti for Roger.

Fire began to tear through the building as Roger closed his eyes in terror. When he opened them, he found himself driving his SUV toward the Pleasant Place Bridge. Roger's imposter turned and looked at Lois in the passenger seat. However, there was something wrong with her. She raised her hands to her throat and squeezed, tighter and tighter. Roger tried to move his hands to help, but they failed to respond. He tried to yell, but his vocal cords were numb. Lois let out a horrid shriek so loud it made his eyes vibrate. Through the ear piercing sound, the vehicle erupted into flames. Lois' skin appeared to melt away to bone as Roger tried to look away, but was unable to move. Suddenly, the sound of knocking began to fill his ears. He anticipated another bizarre vision that would transform his burning vehicle into another sight of terror. His senses screamed as the knocking persisted, and then his mind snapped.

Roger sat up in bed, realizing the images of death and destruction were a lucid dream, the mind's way of exploring his faltering memory synapses. As he returned to the world, banging erupted. Roger sprang to his feet and realized that someone was at his front door. He grabbed the picture of the couple in the park lying on his chest and pushed it into his back pocket. Acting on instinct, he moved to the intruder.

In the entryway, a rhythm of bangs hit the front of the closed door. Roger tiptoed to the peephole, careful to refrain from any fast movements that could signal his presence. He looked through the hole. Distorted like a fisheye lens, he saw two figures who were barely visible. Even with the extreme wide angle, the hat and badges of the trespassers explained their intentions.

"We know you're in there!" barked the officer at the door.

Roger jumped back in fright.

"Shit," he mumbled.

He spun around and noticed the kitchen light still shining brightly as a beacon for the encroaching officers. Roger flipped the switch off and scurried to the rear door. He peered out, checking for any sign of the invading force. The moon lit the backyard as lawn furniture and animal ornaments sprinkled the grass. Roger stepped out as his footsteps vanished into the soft, supportive lawn. He paused, pondering his next move.

The front is blocked, he thought.

To his side was a six-foot cement wall that his overprotective neighbors had constructed.

"No way," he muttered at the immense structure.

To his other side was a waist high, chain-link fence. He concluded that it was a more manageable feat for his body running on a mixture of adrenaline and alcohol. He moved toward the fence, but kicked a hiding flowerpot, toppling it onto the concrete sidewalk. The noise filled the backyard. Roger bit his lip in anger. He didn't waste any time as he plowed over the fence into the neighbor's yard. His momentum continued as he fell into hanging clothes on the line, clutching them for balance. Roger focused on his fingers as he rubbed them together from the noticeable dampness. The neighbor's house was dark and lifeless; the residents seemed to be out-of-town. The middle-aged couple that lived inside traveled frequently for their respective jobs, and often both were away at the same time.

Maybe they forgot their clothes, he thought, but as his memory focused on the swaying fabric, images of last night's action filled his mind.

Roger remembered his sarcastic comment while standing in front of the window. "Her clothes should be dry soon," he had said. Then he remembered Lois' response, "I didn't even know it was supposed to rain today." The thought of rain filled his mind. He remembered the stormy weather from his drive home from work yesterday and his dash from the car holding his umbrella. Fragments of clear thought began to fill a few of the cracks. His after-work shower, dressing in a suit, and Lois' red lipstick all pointed to one fact that was vividly clear to him now.

He murmured his newly recalled fact, "Last night, we had dinner reservations downtown."

9

While Roger had embarked on the most disheartening journey of his life, Lois remained comatose inside her secluded hospital room. Although she lay physically inside the confined room filled with the sound of electronic beeps and scheduled blood pressure pumps, she was actually far, far away. Her mind did not think; it did not react; it did not dream. It was simply dark, but not like the darkness of a cloud-covered night or a lightless room. It was more like the darkness of a bottomless hole, deep in the void of a distant part of the universe where all minds traveled when the lights had gone out.

The door screeched open, adding a new noise to the rhythmic chamber.

"Here she is, sir," the soft voice of Nurse Ann said.

The floor was polished in a high-gloss and, since this particular patient didn't receive any visitors, it remained that way. Nurse Ann's dainty, size six shoes walked into the room, but she was not alone. Behind her reflected a pair of black dress shoes worn by only a man's man. Black dress slacks flowed over the polished shoes and swooshed with each cool glide of the man's step. Hanging at his knees, the bottom of a matching black trench coat encircled the rest of the man's outfit like a shield of styled fabric. Above the shoulders of the coat was the handsome face of Detective Ray Cleveland. He was a striking man, aged gracefully to the prime number of forty-three. Slick black hair covered the top of his dark-featured face, and his green eyes expressed a certain air of power. He was the top detective in his precinct and received more than ten awards of law enforcement excellence handed out personally by the city's mayor. This man knew he wanted to be an officer of law the first moment he could read his father's badge. He knew the career path for him was a detective, a solitary position that required hours of isolation, meticulous investigation, and an intelligent mind. A run-and-gun street cop or paper pusher was definitely not Det. Cleveland's style. He worked alone and preferred to solve a case in his mind first, and then call the cavalry to do the grunt work. He was an Ivy League graduate in the top five percent of his graduating class of Engineering Science majors at the University of Pennsylvania. The detective joined his city's police force following the footsteps of his father and grandfather. He quickly rose to the top of his class at the police academy as his sharp intellectual ability immediately presented itself to his instructors. Det. Cleveland had a logical, mathematical mind and solved his cases by deducing the truth from the facts presented. He didn't believe in magic or the paranormal and knew that every crime had a criminal. The one thing that would always be ingrained in his mind, spoken from his father on his deathbed, was never to get personal with the case. He was adamant about not mixing emotion with commotion and had said, "Think of a case as an engineering problem and all of the variables involved. The wife of the dead husband or the mother of the slain child was just part of the equation." Det. Cleveland kept these words at the front of his mind, but he really didn't need to think about them. They were now instinct, permanently part of his toolbox.

Det. Cleveland was assigned to the "Jane Doe" case, one of many that stemmed from last night's horrific accident. He was at the stage in his career where he could pick and choose the cases he worked on, as his captain gave him that luxury. The case of an unknown person was always a mystery to the detective. Some may say it was part of his ego, but he enjoyed the challenge of finding out the identity of someone no one else could figure out. When he had received the details of the case, the first logical stop was to visit the nameless woman.

Nurse Ann took to Detective Cleveland as soon as he had phoned that he was on his way. She wanted to do whatever she could to help this helpless woman. Nurse Ann found it particularly troubling that someone out there was looking for the fallen angel, and the compassionate nurse had no idea of the emotion consuming that lost individual.

As Det. Cleveland followed Nurse Ann into Lois' room, he filled it with confidence and decisiveness. Nurse Ann sensed it from the moment he had stepped off the elevator and asked for her by name. She could tell that he was a genuine man deep down and one that acted with respect and never arrogance. All her subordinate nurses were female and envious of Nurse Ann assisting handsome police officers during an investigation. Then again, they seemed to warm up to anyone whose masculine cologne tickled their senses.

Det. Cleveland held a notepad and pen as he prepared to takes notes from his commencing investigation. He was old school with certain things. While he used a modern cell phone and laptop to assist his work, he reverted to good old fashioned ink on paper instead of a sometimes-unreliable Personal Digital Assistant. As he walked to Lois' side, his first request was not to look at her unconsciousness body, but her personal belongings retrieved with her lifeless frame. Nurse Ann's quick steps, however, were tough to persuade as he followed the nurse to the woman they knew only as Jane Doe.

"She arrived in the E.R. last night badly injured from the crash on the bridge. It was about ten o'clock. The interesting thing is we don't know who she is. No identification. She was pulled out of the water. Must have been thrown over the bridge from impact," Nurse Ann explained as the detective gravitated to her side.

Her last words made her quiver, as startling flashes of speculative terror on the bridge filled her mind. Det. Cleveland remained detached and aloof. He jotted some keywords down in his notepad, "E.R. ten o'clock" and "No identification." He underlined the latter because it was a troublesome fact of the case. He momentarily pondered his ability to solve the case, but images of his many detective awards quickly reassured him.

If I can solve a missing child's case, surely I can figure out who this woman is and where she belongs, he reasoned.

Confidence was the number one asset any good detective needed and Det. Cleveland was full of it, but in a pure, respectful way—never to the point of pretentiousness.

"What was the subject wearing when you brought her in?" Det. Cleveland asked.

"Just what was left of her black dress. We have it with her personal items…" Nurse Ann responded, but ended the sentence short. She tried to think if Jane Doe had arrived with anything as most unknown patients were admitted with at least some identifiable items— usually enough to jumpstart a pursuing officer. However, she realized this sleeping woman entered the hospital with nothing—as if she were from an unknown world.

Nurse Ann finished her sentence, "...actually that's all we have for her. She had nothing else on her."

Det. Cleveland lifted his pen, as he had nothing to write down. He hoped the dainty nurse would've said that Jane Doe arrived with a purse filled with unique perfume, a movie ticket stub, or even a dry cleaning receipt. Unfortunately, she didn't mention any such items that could possibly have shed light on the dark situation. Det. Cleveland tried to turn the bad news around and use the lack of clues as a clue itself.

"Hmm, must have been at a party...or nice restaurant for dinner. She probably was with a date," he deduced aloud.

Det. Cleveland took another moment to formulate his thoughts. "A fancy dress would certainly not have pockets, which therefore only allowed a handbag for her personal belongings," he added.

With the jarring accident on the bridge, who knew where the small item was in the rubbish or even the water? The one thing his gut told him was that she was most likely not alone in the traveling car, as her slimming dress would most probably be to delight the senses of a date. With statistics in favor of a heterosexual relationship, he calculated the person accompanying her was male, a boyfriend or husband, and this person was most likely her chauffeur. This was his first piece to the freshly cut jigsaw puzzle.

"Okay, thank you for the information. I have enough for some leads," he said.

Det. Cleveland jotted down some of his conjectures into his notepad as Nurse Ann focused on Lois. She took her warm hand and compassionately caressed the skin of Lois' cheek. It was cold at first, but the heat from Nurse Ann quickly heated the spot. Det. Cleveland clicked his pen and put his notepad and writing utensil into his trench coat. He knew that Nurse Ann was having a moment, and he didn't want to make eye contact. In fact, he couldn't because he knew that keeping the nameless woman a variable in the overall equation was the best way to maintain his success at detecting. Having no emotional involvement would be the best approach to solving the case, and he knew this was going to be a much harder one to crack. This mentality kept the brazen man fresh and probably explained why he rarely had any time to date, let alone find someone who could put up with his particular way of thinking.

Nurse Ann didn't let up from her empathy, which made Det. Cleveland uncomfortable. He wanted to end the conversation, but was respectful enough not to simply walk away. He knew he had to say something.

"Will the woman be okay?" he finally said, ending the silence.

"I guess you could say the worst is behind her. She just needs to pull through this coma."

Nurse Ann turned as Det. Cleveland grinned at her, not looking at the sleeping beauty. Finally, she led him out of the room as he eagerly followed. They stepped into the hall as the door to Lois' lair closed, sealing her inside until another visitor.

"Thank you, again. Please let me know if her status changes. Here is my card with my direct cell number. I hope she awakens to solve this conundrum," Det. Cleveland said as he handed the nurse his business card.

Nurse Ann graciously accepted it. She trusted Det. Cleveland even though he showed no emotion, the way one trusted a surgeon to remove a brain tumor.

A focused man is a man who gets things done, she thought. The thing that needed to be done needed to be done quickly, accurately, and brazenly.

"You're welcome, sir. I am the fifth floor head nurse. Please let me know how I can help," she responded as she offered her hand.

"I will certainly let you know of any updates," Det. Cleveland replied cordially.

Both departed, going separate ways on the floor. A sudden silence engulfed the hallway. Faintly, the sound of Lois' beating heart resonated through her room's closed door.

After a few minutes, Det. Cleveland walked off the busy elevator into the lobby. Thoughts of his best approach to the case were racing through his logical mind. He was trying to sort things out like a computer sorting a jumbled array. Det. Cleveland knew the first step was to check for Jane Doe's potential mate from the accident. Hopefully, he thought, the man was alive and could shed light on the puzzling situation. Det. Cleveland stopped in the hallway on his way to his parked car. He was anxious to check with his research assistant back at his precinct. The young man's name was Charlie, and he was a great tool in Det. Cleveland's toolbox, providing wonders with database query searches and cross-department interviews. When Det. Cleveland tasked Charlie with an action item, the researcher gave his heart to accomplish the task, and above all, was loyal to the venerable detective. Det. Cleveland lived by the adage "actions speak louder than words" and this proved Charlie's trustworthiness during the early part of their relationship. In the middle of a heated murder investigation, the precinct's captain grilled the entire office about Det. Cleveland's methods of interrogating a murder suspect. Det. Cleveland knew the man was the culprit and pressed him during the heated examination. Charlie had been taking notes through the one-way glass and, when asked by the captain, he covered for Det. Cleveland and simply said, "I didn't see anything against policy."

The side hallway was secluded as Det. Cleveland speed dialed Charlie.

"Yello," Charlie slanged as he sat at his desk consumed with mountains of paperwork.

"Hey, Charlie. I stopped by Southern General to follow up on that Jane Doe. She's still in a coma and unconscious. Uh, can you pull up all cars involved in yesterday's crash? I'm looking for a man involved. Could be her boyfriend or husband," the detective asked as he glanced in his notepad.

The police station buzzed with the evening shift holding down the fort. The night seemed to bring out the worst in a city; the petty criminals, drunks, and hoodlums all crawled out of the woodwork. Being low on the totem pole, Charlie sat near the front of the building, which was a frequently traveled path for entry by the front line police force to the rear of the cramped station. This was where the leadership hung their hats, but even their offices were not much bigger than a poor family's broom closet.

Charlie leaned in to the seclusion of his desk and confided, "Actually, we had the strangest thing happen. Saint Peters North had a Roger Belkin who was injured in the crash. He had some pretty bad head trauma. Well apparently, he just got up and walked right out of the hospital, nobody even stopped him. He stole a car from the lot, and was last seen at his home."

Det. Cleveland widened his eyes as his heart rate incited.

"Oh, really. What's his address?"

Charlie knew Det. Cleveland was anxious to trek forward on the case. He focused on his computer screen and managed the mouse and keyboard like an artist using a brush and palette to paint his masterpiece. An incident report popped up on the screen with a plethora of investigative data. The title of the screen read "Belkin, Roger – Incident." Charlie scrolled toward the bottom to find the needle in the haystack.

"One Thirty Three Dietrich Road," Charlie replied.

Det. Cleveland marked the information in his notepad, and then thanked Charlie.

Just as he was ready to close his phone, Charlie quickly interjected, "Anything for you, man. Mr. Workaholic. We gotta get you out on the town and hit the bar district."

The twenty-seven-year-old was always trying to break the focused detective's seemingly impenetrable shell. Det. Cleveland thought about having a few drinks with Charlie and the crew from time to time. Maybe it would do him good. However, when he had finished a case or even part of a case, something else always arose which kept the detective incapable of finding any time to socialize, even if he contrived this something else.

"Bye, Charlie," Det. Cleveland responded as he shook his head smugly.

"Call if you need anything," Charlie responded.

Det. Cleveland closed his cell phone and took a moment to collect his thoughts. He thought about this man named Roger Belkin, a man who just walked out of a hospital and took matters into his own hands to get home.

Why did he do such a thing? he thought. *Was it out of disregard for the law, complete arrogance, or a repercussion from the accident on the Pleasant Place Bridge?* Det. Cleveland could not fathom how it must have been to experience the turmoil from the fiery crash last night. He could not answer these questions, even with all of his focused skills as a detective. The next step was clear to him—find the man with some answers.

I wonder what this Belkin is up to, he pondered before he exited the hospital.

10

The sky was dark and the road was full of life. Lois' big sister, Carol, drove her modest sedan toward the city. She was going to do some shopping at a quaint organic food store downtown. Carol was a homemaker. While some may have looked at the job as second-rate, she looked at it like a career. Carol enjoyed tending to the home, washing clothes, dusting, and preparing dinner. She liked a clean habitat and enjoyed sharing it with her husband, Robert, who respected Carol's choice in their marriage. However, no lives were perfect. The one thing hers lacked was a child, a little person to care for, to teach, and to love. It was not by choice, as she and her husband had spent almost a year of old pregnancy wives' tales, but she soon received the terrifying truth. Her doctor explained it was a genetic defect in her ovary and the bottom line was that she could not conceive a child. Even with modern medical science, drugs, or surgery, there was nothing possible to change nature. That was about ten years ago. Carol and Robert considered adopting, but after a long, hard discussion, they chose to adopt a newly born beagle they named Lucy. The playful canine was their "child" and it filled the void. This left Carol even more protective of her younger sister, Lois. Carol was almost like another parent, not in the least bit condescending, but in a shielding way. Since their parents were retired and lived out of state, Carol made sure that she was there whenever her baby sister needed her.

As Carol drove, she thought about Lois' date the previous night. The sisters would usually talk daily on the phone or during a visit, but it was not uncommon for a day to pass here or there without contact if one or both of them had been busy. After all, they were grown, married women. Carol figured that Lois and Roger had arrived home late last night after a lavish evening out and had a playful nightcap before an intimate encounter. Carol liked Roger, not just for his financial stability and honor, but also for the protection he offered her sister. She remembered one time how Roger called home as he usually did around lunchtime, but there was no answer from Lois. To make sure his wife was unharmed, he left work and sped home, only to find Lois taking a nap with the phone's ringer accidently turned off. Carol knew her sister was safe with Roger. Even though Lois would sometimes complain about her husband's forgetfulness,

Carol was certain that Roger would never forget to protect her.

Carol had a busy morning and afternoon with the bi-yearly bedroom "deep cleaning," as she liked to call it. It consisted of stripping their king-sized bed, washing the sheets, and then flipping the mattress. This was just the start of her work as she vacuumed the entire room by moving the dressers and night stands to pulverize the hiding dust mites. Robert didn't like that Carol performed all of the shifting and moving by herself, but her adamant behavior was hard to change. This left her with little time to watch the news or even to read the paper, something she usually did in the morning. Robert was going to be working late at his corporate sales job, which left Carol to dine alone. She had a craving for a dish she made last month after she had read the recipe on the Internet. It was a baked black bean burrito filled with roasted chicken, steamed rice, fresh tomatoes, and a touch of basil. She had all of the ingredients except for the most important one—the black beans. The recipe required four ounces of black beans and the downtown organic specialty store had a naturally grown organic variety, perfect for her holistic way of eating. This was Carol's reason for her voyage. By her calculations, it would be a short fifteen-minute drive into the city, ten minutes at the grocer, and then fifteen minutes back. This, of course, was dependent on minimal traffic and a close parking spot, but even in the worst case, she figured, it would be an hour tops for the trip.

Carol was nearing the passageway required to gain access to the city, the Pleasant Place Bridge, and she hoped traffic was moving quickly. The structure of the bridge came into her view. Its tall wire suspensions connected the two towers reaching for the sky. As she approached, she saw flashing red and blue lights from emergency vehicles in the middle of the bridge. At first, she thought a fender-bender was the reason for the emergency crew or even a crazed jumper. However, she realized two of the emergency vehicles were parked in the middle of the lanes, which prevented any traffic.

"What's going on?" she mumbled.

Up ahead, two police cars blocked the entryway onto the bridge with a younger traffic cop standing guard. Only a few vehicles scattered the roadway, which was strange for the usually bustling bridge.

Did I miss something? she pondered.

As her senses surrendered to the mystery, Carol neared the traffic cop and rolled down her window.

"What's going on?" she asked.

"You didn't hear, ma'am? There was a huge pile up last night on the bridge. It was a mess, but we're almost done cleaning it up," he responded apathetically.

Carol raised her hand to her mouth. She wondered how she had missed such a prominent story. Her day of intense cleaning must have been the reason for not catching the news. She didn't read the newspaper, didn't watch television, and didn't talk to Lois or her husband. In fact, she realized she didn't talk to anyone all day.

Surely, she reasoned, this story would've been the first thing out of someone's mouth who was from the city.

"Was anyone hurt?" Carol asked.

"Yeah, several died actually," the traffic cop said.

His gaze transferred to the cars waiting behind Carol's parked vehicle.

"Uh, you're going to have to find an alternate route. We need to keep this area clear," he instructed.

Carol was stunned. She looked at the colossal bridge built for a fleet of speeding vehicles, but all she saw was a traffic-less shell. The normally thriving structure appeared lifeless. There was an ominous aura radiating from it.

A sudden feeling of loneliness overwhelmed Carol. She yearned for someone to explain the situation, someone who shared the same exasperation that she felt. She thought of Lois. She wanted more than anything to speak to her little sister.

11

The night air was cool and brisk. Roger staggered alongside a lightly driven road toward a shopping district. He was destined for the downtown some ten miles away, traveling the shortest route, which included the Pleasant Place Bridge. As Roger walked, a few passing cars honked their horns at the man they assumed was nothing more than an unstable bum. This, however, didn't stop Roger's drive as his mind and body focused on reaching the heart of the city to rebuild his memory.

This road was the one that Roger drove every time he had traveled into the city to work. From his current angle, the highway appeared unfamiliar. The upper-middle-class man had never actually walked the road, which made him second-guess his charted course. After about a mile, his right leg began to hurt again. Each abnormal step caused his left leg's knee, the better one, to bend unnaturally, which induced more fatigue in his ailing body. He calculated it was the fact that his liver had finally removed his body's painkiller—the alcohol. Roger began to lose sight of the downtown. His burning drive to uncover more pieces of the puzzle was quickly fading from a blazing fire to a candle flame starving for wax. Roger recognized his idea to walk was brainless, and he knew he had to do or find something quickly.

Should I hitchhike? he wondered.

Roger figured it was a viable option. He saw a car's headlights racing toward him, but as he raised his arm to gesture the world-recognized "thumbs up," a sharp pain traversed his bicep. The car flew by, nearly blowing Roger off the road. He was in bad shape and was quickly getting worse. His immediate goal was to find a way to kill the pain receptors in his exhausted brain.

Up ahead, Roger saw lights in the distance. It was the trite gas station he always passed on a ride into the city. He never stopped at the business because it always looked like the type of place robbed more than a bank with an open vault. However, it was a place to rest. Tall oak trees obstructed the full view of the store, but the blinding sign lit the sky like the constellation Orion. Roger stumbled toward the structure. The sign finally revealed itself, "Raj's Quick Mart."

The place was small with only four gasoline pumps in front and a diesel station on the side. No cars filled their tanks, probably due to the overpriced fuel grades. However, several cars were parked outside the convenience store as well as a large tractor-trailer lacking its load stationed near the diesel pump. Roger made it to the door as he sighed with relief under the bright lights of the canopy. The intense radiance hurt his sensitive eyes, but he saw the inside was even brighter.

Roger entered the compact store. Six aisles stacked with junk food, trinkets, and soda offered patrons a choice of the bare necessities of life and nothing more. The clerk was none other than Raj himself, the owner and operator originally from Pakistan with a stereotypical Middle-Eastern English accent. As soon as Roger entered his store, the owner's eyes swiftly studied what he perceived as a potentially troublesome beggar. Quirky music from another decade belted from a cassette player near Raj's side. In front of him, an elderly woman was indulging herself with a daily dose of lottery tickets.

"That'll be four dollar," Raj rasped.

The woman handed the man four crisp bills from her recently cashed Social Security check and proceeded to exit the store. As she did, her eyes filled with the image of Roger's incapacitated frame. She let out an instinctive gasp as Roger scanned the store for a cure to his uncommon cold.

"Where is your aspirin?" Roger asked the suspicious owner.

"Aisle three," the man replied with his chin held high.

Roger suddenly stopped cold. He stood in front of a large display of bottled water directly adjacent to a small section of automotive products. A seemingly innocuous bottle of fuel injector cleaner was the object entrancing Roger. It wasn't so much the item, as it was the writing on the label. "Dynamite Fuel Injector Cleaner" was plastered on the side. Roger's mind shifted to his lost wife. He thought of the way her hair flowed in the breeze and how she subtly raised her eyebrow from one of his witty jokes. His mind was removed from his body as he stood there absorbed by a single word.

Suddenly, a pop erupted from behind the register. Raj bent to pick up a phone book he had accidently knocked to the floor. While the noise was abrupt, the patrons did nothing more than give a quick glance toward its origin. However, Roger did something much more than just shift his eyes. His oversensitive mind, lost in another world, reacted strongly to the impromptu noise. His brain triggered a surge to the muscles throughout his body, sending him off his feet and into the bottled water display behind him. Bottles burst and rolled throughout the confined store. A couple deciding between cheese fries and barbecue chips peered over aisle five toward the outburst.

"Okay. Okay. Get out! Get out my store!" Raj demanded. His suspicions panned out.

Roger picked himself up and hustled toward the exit.

"Leave my store," the owner added as Roger moved past him.

"Ah. Calm down. Calm down," a boisterous voice bellowed from somewhere.

As Roger reached the door, the man attached to the voice revealed himself. He was a tall, hefty fellow about fifty years old and seemed to be on the side of the American-born man. His name was Jack and he was the driver of the monstrous truck parked near the diesel-pump.

Roger collected himself under the bright lights outside the door as Jack gave him a big, friendly pat on the back, which nearly knocked him to the ground.

"Ah, these dune coons. They come to our country and don't even have the brotherly love to give a good guy a break. Don't worry about him," the loud trucker roared.

Jack was the type of man who said what he felt even if it wasn't politically correct. He liked to drive a tractor-trailer for the sense of power and respect on the road that the magnificent vehicle demanded. Jack traveled the country in his power wagon and frequently stopped off at strip clubs and dive bars, and was proud of it. He had filled his diesel tank up and was browsing the beer specials when fate seemed to bring Roger and him together.

"Hey. You look like shit, man," Jack remarked with a chuckle as he studied Roger.

Roger nodded.

"Where's the flood? Ha! I couldn't resist," he added as he glanced at Roger's ankle-high pants. "Jack's the name," he said, offering his sturdy hand.

"Roger," the businessman replied as he instinctively gripped it.

Roger's mind entrenched the action from his high-profile job, the job that seemed to be in another chapter of a partially burned book. Roger somehow felt a sense of relief in the presence of this man. His worries appeared to get a temporary push aside. He knew he would never have met this type of character in his real life and there was no way to explain how he reached this moment in his journey thus far. But the trucker's force and conviction seemed to be just what Roger needed. Let someone on his current level stand up and offer his hand, Roger figured.

"Hey, where's your ride?" Jack asked as he scanned the nearly deserted lot.

Roger didn't know how to answer the question because he didn't even know the location of his black SUV. For all he knew, it could be in the same place where his lost wife was hiding.

Roger's lack of response didn't stop Jack from offering his help. "You must be a nomad. I can see that... Do you need a lift?" the trucker solicited.

"Um. Well..." Roger muttered as he perked up. He realized his search for a ride presented itself in an unusual way, but he was glad the trucker offered.

"Come on," Jack said.

Jack took the lead and walked toward his truck. He strolled with a limp on his right leg and moved slowly because of it, which was just the right speed for Roger.

"We got the ol' war wagon here. I'm heading into the city. Got to drop it back off and get my check. I'm just finishing up from a week's trip," Jack explained.

The venerable truck presented itself on the side of the gas station. It was dark, dirty, and meaty as Jack waved his hand presenting it like a model on a game show. Roger neared the grill and immediately took in the word "Mack" and the famous Bulldog emblem proudly plastered on the front. Jack banged on the hood as he smiled with pride. This was the trucker's job, his home, and his life, and he was anxious to share it with a weary, fellow traveler.

As Roger approached the grill, he noticed remnants of dried blood and fur stuck in the truck's teeth.

"Damn varmints. They don't stand a chance against this here beast. Hah!" Jack added with zest. Then he yelled, "Hop in."

Jack walked around to the captain's chair as Roger moved to the passenger's side. He noticed a confederate flag proudly flapping in the night air, which seemed fitting for the against-the-grain truck driver.

Roger hopped up into the truck's cabin. The throbbing pain in his leg and arm, which had driven him to the gas station, was suddenly alleviated. He didn't need aspirin or even more alcohol to cure his aches; he simply needed the companionship of someone on his level. While Roger didn't exactly know this trucker's true identity, he was glad that Jack's helping hand seemed to block the pain.

The cabin was cool with a slight smell of some sort of masculine stench. Roger glanced behind him and saw a single bed with adult magazines scattered on top. He realized this was really the man's home on the road, which explained the foul smell only produced from the griminess of an unkempt male's room.

"Let's blow this joint," Jack yelled as he started the semi.

The powerful twelve-cylinder diesel roared to life. It rocked the cabin with its idle as Jack gave the animal a few revs to clear its throat. Roger watched as Jack smiled with each push of the throttle. As the monster howled, the trucker looked at Roger and nodded his head in acceptance.

"Feel that power. Succumb to it. Make love to it."

Jack maneuvered the gears and took charge of the truck. As he pulled out, a sudden motion in the side view mirror caught Roger's attention. He saw Raj, the Middle-Eastern clerk, flailing his arms with a look of rage consuming his face.

"Did you pay for the gas?" Roger asked.

"Screw this place! I'll never come back here. That guy can shove it."

With those words, Roger shook his head. He knew that Jack really was going against-the-grain with his actions. However, his actions at least proved that Jack was a man with principles. Roger was glad the trucker was on his side.

Jack power-shifted the truck with elegant grace, like a perfectly choreographed ballroom dance. He was the lead and the steering wheel, shifter, clutch, and gas pedal were collectively his eager partner.

The storeowner ran with all of his energy but saw the powerful machine had a clear advantage, the advantage of horsepower. He had one of the bottled waters from Roger's bout with the display. Realizing he had lost the battle, the clerk threw the bottle in desperation. It bounced off the semi's armor, and then burst on the ground, covering the macadam with water.

The truck plowed forward on the night road. Off in the distance, a faint glow from the city lights radiated in the sky. With danger behind them, Roger glanced around the cabin and analyzed the trucker's home. Suggestive pictures of naked women, the scruffy man's female companions, were plastered within his immediate view. Junk food wrappers and crumpled newspapers covered the floor like the bleachers following a sold-out baseball game. Roger could understand the pornographic images and refuse, but the item that was stuck to the dashboard seemed bizarrely out of place. An alligator bobble head doll, staring at the duo, chattered with each jostle of the truck.

"Where did you get that?" Roger asked.

"On the road, when I was passing through Florida. I hit a rest stop off the ninety-five. It was dark and late and I remember hopping down from the truck, and there he was."

"Who?" Roger asked as he squinted his eyes, intrigued beyond his wits like a kid in the middle of his grandfather's war story.

"A gator. He had to be twelve feet long lurking there in the darkness. He lunged at me but I wrestled him down. I had his head around my arm in the Anaconda Vice." Jack curled his arm simulating the move.

"You wrestled in high school?" Roger asked.

"No. I like to watch women's wrastlin' on TV," Jack replied with a smile.

Roger chuckled. He was holding the barbaric man on too high of a pedestal, as he only knew the road and had unique street smarts that were beyond Roger.

"Anyway, he was a fighter. I could see it in his eyes. He had those crazy eyes," Jack added.

"Crazy eyes?" Roger muttered. He realized the trucker's dictionary consisted of bizarre sayings and obscure definitions.

"He was a powerful bugger. We flipped around on the ground. I stunned him and went for the pile driver, but he took a chunk out of me," Jack continued.

Roger's mouth dropped, but he couldn't have predicted what the trucker was going to do next. Jack reached down, grabbed his pants leg, and lifted it to reveal a prosthetic foot attached to his ankle.

"After that, he took off like he was the winner in the Belt Match...and that's why I got that bobble head. Kind of a parting gift from Florida."

"You wrestled an alligator? You *wrestled* an alligator?" Roger added in awe. He mouthed to himself, "Who the hell is this guy?"

Roger thought that if someone had told him yesterday he would be driving shotgun in a meaty tractor-trailer with a loud, foot-less man, he would have called him crazy. This proved his life was no longer predicable. If that person he would have called crazy had actually predicted this exact situation, Roger would have asked him his most burning question, "Where is she?"

Jack continued to babble about his life on the road as the city lights grew brighter with each passing moment. Roger suddenly felt sleepy, a feeling he experienced only when he had felt safe and in-control of his surroundings. For the first time since he had awoken into this nightmare, he felt a hint of security. Roger wished that if he closed his eyes, he would not fall asleep, but fall awake and turn this bizarre dream into a clear reality.

12

The road ahead was dark. Det. Cleveland was on his way toward the Belkin house hoping to find the clues he needed to answer the question, "Who is Jane Doe?" As the detective drove alone in his sedan, a pair of bright headlights illuminated the oncoming lane. They were higher than a normal car's lights and were spaced apart a foot or two wider than the average automobile. As the speeding vehicle approached, Det. Cleveland realized it was a tractor-trailer. If he only knew that the man with the answer to his question, and the man who needed the detective to answer his own, was in that powerful vehicle, the story would be over. The vehicles passed each other. For an instant, the two men were side-by-side. Nevertheless, how would they know of this ironic passing? It was nothing more than speeding cars traveling in opposite directions, something all people experienced in their daily lives on the road. If one stops to ponder the existence of the hundreds, even thousands, of passing vehicles encountered in any given day, the answer to many questions could be in one of those passing cars. These ironic situations occurred all of the time, but if one was not aware of their existence, does the irony, in fact, still exist?

Det. Cleveland arrived at the Belkin home. It was larger than he had expected and the affluent neighborhood said a lot about the man he was trying to question. As the detective pulled up alongside the curb, a mufflerless tow truck backed up from the driveway towing Roger's heisted get-away vehicle. Det. Cleveland noticed two black-and-whites parked in the driveway as a tall, muscular patrolman watched the tow truck drive away. Det. Cleveland stepped out from his handsome sedan and walked toward the muscular patrolman.

"Detective Ray Cleveland from the south precinct...What did you guys find?" the detective asked as he flipped his police badge.

"Well, the guy skipped out. We figured he'd come back here after he stole a car from Saint Peters North Hospital. The owner is pretty pissed off."

"Did you find anything in the house?" Det. Cleveland asked as he took in the sizable structure.

He felt dwarfed by the immense house, as its spacious two-stories housed a living area easily three times his own.

The muscular patrolman followed the detective's gaze, and then replied, "I don't think so. We're just finishing up our search. Ha! The nerve of this guy. This is a story for the guys back at the office."

The patrolman turned the conversation from professional to personal. Det. Cleveland knew that, until the case was solved, there was no time for pointless jests or personal opinions.

"Thanks for the update," he replied.

The patrolman stepped back toward his squad car as Det. Cleveland gravitated toward the front door, which was wide open with the downstairs' lights on.

Det. Cleveland stepped through the front door. He swept his eyes around the entryway as he always had done when searching for clues. Nothing was insignificant when it came to investigating a case. He remembered the time when the evidence in a narcotics case was hidden on top of a cupboard, and his keen eyes noticed the tail of the string used to pull it down. Finding the location wasn't a unique accomplishment, but the fact that he found it during his first pass of the apartment was unusual, as it would have puzzled most rookie detectives looking only for the obvious.

His scan of the entryway didn't answer any questions, but did provide crucial exposition to the man wanted for questioning. The affluence certainly suggested the man didn't heist due to lack of money and implied he had a much stronger motive, one driven by a deeper human emotion. As Det. Cleveland looked around, he heard the banter of two men. They talked about a fellow officer's follies on a police chase through the downtown streets. Det. Cleveland walked toward the location of the voices, the kitchen.

The lights brightly burned as Det. Cleveland sneaked up on the two men. One was a skinny, twenty-eight-year-old patrolman whose uniform seemed two sizes too big. He had jet-black hair and a small mustache that looked unnatural on his boyish face. The other patrolman was thirty and had a round belly like Santa Clause. Opposite of St. Nick's white hair, his head was shaved with a few days' stubble poking through his scalp, which revealed his receding hairline. Both were inspecting Roger's liquor cabinet. The sight of the detective widened their eyes, as if they were kids with their hands in a cookie jar.

"Oh. Sorry, sir," said the husky patrolman as he and his accomplice set down their respective bottles.

"Detective Ray Cleveland," the detective replied as he flashed his badge. "At ease gentlemen. What do you got?"

"He has a nice collection of rums," the skinny patrolman blurted.

"No, you ass, he means the house," rasped the burly man.

Det. Cleveland remained emotionless on the outside, but he was rolling his eyes in his mind.

"Oh. Well, we searched it. It looks like he was either in the house and left, or he was never here in the first place. We gave everything a once-over," the skinny patrolman explained.

"Any sign of struggle or other anomalies?"

"No, sir. We are about done here anyway. They're going to send a car by for a stake-out," the scrawny patrolman continued.

Det. Cleveland realized these first responders were worthless to him. He did give them credit for checking the immediacy of the situation and for taking care of returning the stolen car to its owner, but they lacked the killer instinct that only a well-bred detective could offer.

"I see. Thanks, guys. I'm going to give the place a walk through. I'll lock up," Det. Cleveland responded.

The two patrolmen removed their gaze from the prominent detective and walked past him with their heads held low. They resembled mischievous schoolboys leaving the principal's office after being drilled with questions. Det. Cleveland heard the door shut behind him, which quickly brought silence into the spacious house. He walked over to the liquor cabinet, the structure that intrigued the two immature patrolmen. Several bottles of rum and brandy lined the top, but the large jug of wine that dominated the other inferior bottles caught his attention. Det. Cleveland picked up the jug and winced from its hefty weight. The label revealed it as Lambrusco. While the detective did not have much knowledge of wine, he figured this must have been a delicacy for the residents of the home.

Det. Cleveland set the bottle down and turned to take in the kitchen. He walked slowly toward the window above the sink. It was as if he tried to mask the echo of his footsteps, but the hardwood floors provided no cushion to his posh dress shoes. Det. Cleveland peered through the window and noticed the swaying clothes hanging on the neighbor's line. The fabric's movement was soft and slow from the night breeze and it took some strength to remove his eyes from the hypnotic motion. After a minute, the detective turned and moved toward a floral arrangement. The daisies, tulips, and lilacs were still glowing and vibrant, which suggested to him that they had received a drink not more than thirty-six hours ago. Det. Cleveland walked toward the exit of the kitchen, and then flipped the light switch. He paused for a moment as his mind suddenly went blank. It was as if he couldn't think or move. Little did the detective know, he was standing in the precise spot as the man he was trying to locate with the same radiating glow silhouetting his body from the entryway light. The only difference, however, was that he faced the opposite way that Roger had faced earlier in the evening.

The sound of Det. Cleveland's footsteps changed tone as he moved onto the older hardwood floors. Roger had remodeled the kitchen last year with new flooring and the entryway still had the original wood from the house's construction some ten years ago. The detective, however, had no way of knowing this, and if he somehow found Roger hiding upstairs, the reason his footsteps sounded differently would probably be the last question he would ask.

Det. Cleveland looked up the stairway before ascending. He always looked and assessed before he did anything, even just walking up stairs. The hallway was dark, but the light from the master bedroom immediately drew his attention. He pondered whether the front-line officers had left the light illuminated or whether it had been the owner of the house before his great escape.

Det. Cleveland stood at the doorway to the master bedroom. He took in the queen-sized bed in the center with nightstands on each side. He moved into the room. Immediately, the smell of alcohol tickled his nose. Det. Cleveland looked on top of the counters, but nothing that would have emitted the smell revealed itself. Checking the next probable location, he looked at the base of the bed, moving the flowing skirt on each side. Then he found the culprit—a bottle of "Jack Daniel's Old Tennessee Whiskey." Det. Cleveland put the bottle on the nightstand and looked at the side of the bed next to him. The covers were slightly imprinted on one side and near the pillow, just enough for the detective to confirm that a body had recently rested on top of the bed. He assumed the officers did not tamper with the light and the signs therefore suggested that Mr. Belkin, the owner, had used alcohol as a downer to induce sleep. Then, he had exercised the side of the bed as his resting place closest to the bottle. Det. Cleveland conjectured that when the patrolmen had startled him awake from the front door, Roger

Belkin fled through the path of least resistance, the back door. Det. Cleveland made note of this in his notepad, trying to put a timeline and sequence to the man's actions.

The bathroom behind him begged inspection. Although Det. Cleveland was anxious to check out the backyard for clues, he knew he had to exhaust the immediate area to look for a smoking gun. He walked into the dark bathroom, flipping the light switch. He caressed the towel hanging over the shower door. Toiletries lined the back of the clean toilet and sink. The lipstick case caught the detective's eyes as he gravitated toward the seemingly innocuous object. He wondered whether this was, in fact, the lipstick used by the unconscious Jane Doe lying in Southern General Hospital. As he looked at the woman's make-up, his eyes shifted to the mirror in front of him. He paused, staring at his cool mug peering back at him. He looked at his dark eyebrows and green eyes. The man staring back appeared in-control and collected, but there was a slight wrinkle on his skin under his left eye. Det. Cleveland did not notice it before, but something about the concentrated lighting brought out all of the reflection's flaws. Even though the wrinkle was subtle, it made Det. Cleveland question the man staring at him. He suddenly felt older and no longer impenetrable. The wrinkle signified a chink in his armor and made him think about death. There must have been something about this mirror, he finally concluded, something that made him see things he had never seen before. He thought about Roger Belkin standing in the same spot and wondered how many answers to his questions the all-seeing mirror had concealed.

Det. Cleveland turned and left the confines of the bathroom. He flipped the switch, leaving the small space in darkness. He moved toward the master bedroom door as his steps created a filtered "clump" on the carpet. As he turned off the light switch, he hesitated with his hand still resting on the plastic toggle. His mind thought about any other clues he may have missed. As his brain calculated, his gut told him there was something else in the room, something that he had overlooked. Det. Cleveland flipped the switch back on. He gave the room another once over, and then it became clear. He galloped toward the pictures on the nightstand. A photograph behind a phone burned into his view. He grabbed it and saw a man smiling with a bubbly woman in his arms. He took a moment to assess the female, and then realized the animated woman was the same lifeless body alone in Nurse Ann's care.

"Jane Doe!" he exclaimed.

He was baffled by how an attractive and vivacious woman who radiated from a piece of glossy paper could transform into an inanimate object with a grim future. He studied the good-looking man holding the woman. The man looked content and blissful as he embraced her. Det. Cleveland took a moment to put himself in the shoes of the photographer. The couple stood in front of the gigantic Hoover Dam, proud to share the moment together. A pair of birds soared in the blue sky above them. Then, Det. Cleveland shifted his eyes toward the bottom of the picture and saw written, "Roger and his *Dynamite* Lois."

Det. Cleveland grabbed the picture frame. He received the burning answer to his question of Jane Doe's identity. She was Lois Belkin, wife to Roger Belkin of One Thirty Three Dietrich Road. He thought about Roger, a family man who lived in a perfect house in a perfect neighborhood, and wondered where this seemingly perfect man was at this moment. He wished he could tell him where his wife was and how to see her, but he could not do that at the moment. Det. Cleveland set the picture down and headed out of the room, eager to get this newly acquired information to those who needed it.

13

The purr of the tractor-trailer rhythmically rocked the powerful beast. The V-12 diesel was low, hypnotic, and enough to put someone to sleep, which was exactly what had happened to Roger. Jack glanced over and saw the weary man's head tilted and his eyes closed. His mouth was slightly open, and his chest swayed with each breath. He wondered about Roger.

"Where did this man come from?" he asked himself under his breath, but then he thought about the unwritten rule of the road—a traveler's past should remain his past without judgment.

While Roger appeared peaceful sitting on the urine-stained vinyl seat, his mind was under duress. It saw vivid, disjointed images juxtaposed in a way that created a trapped world of terror. Roger was back at the serene lake sitting on a blanket with the love of his life. Birds chirped in the flowing trees and the warm sun glistened off the placid lake. Roger felt protected as the lucid image of Lois made this dream worth experiencing, but again, he was paralyzed. He could see his wife in perfect clarity, her soft hair, spongy skin, and innocent smile, but as he tried to reach out and touch her, his hand failed to respond. Lois grabbed a small hors d'oeuvre and took a dainty bite. As the image soothed Roger's senses, his wife reached into the basket and unearthed two sparkling glasses. She grasped a bottle of deep red wine and, while Roger couldn't see the label, he knew it was Lambrusco. Lois poured two glasses and handed one to Roger, a spectator in his own dream. Both tipped glasses with a "tink" and sipped the ripened wine. Roger felt powerless by not having physical control of his body. However, the image of the woman he had so desperately craved was all that mattered. He gazed into her brown eyes, which glimmered in the sun like a fresh pile of autumn leaves. Just as his focus was on the perfect image of his college sweetheart, clouds quickly stole the sunlight from her face. Light became dark, bright became dim, and life became death as the sky rapidly grew into a morose mess. Thunder crashed and a bolt of lightning electrified the water. Roger trembled. He tried to speak, to move, and even to look away, but he was forced to endure the terrifying experience. Lois' smile turned into a frown. Her eyes widened and her eyebrows heightened as her expression changed into a look of horror. Rain dumped down and soaked Lois' dress. Her hair transformed into a clumped mess and her hint of eye make-up ran down her cheek like black tears. Lois bolted from the blanket. Roger tried to fight the paralysis, but it prevailed. He watched as Lois darted behind a massive oak tree. As his senses screamed, thunder crashed again, pulsating Roger's incapacitated body. Then, a bolt of electricity sparked the top of the oak trees.

"Roger, come find me. Please Roger, find me," a ghostly voice of Lois uttered from somewhere.

Lois was gone from Roger's view. She was lost in an image of panic. Suddenly, he saw the intense lights of the angry sky. It overwhelmed his sore eyes with light so bright it was no longer light.

The lights quickly transformed into bright headlights in an oncoming lane of a highway. Roger sprang awake from his impossible nightmare and blinked his eyes rapidly. He was in the moment just after awakening when dreams and reality blurred. His other senses began to rouse. The concocted smell of body odor, rotting food, and diesel fumes provoked his nose. Then, Jack's deep voice filled Roger's ears.

"Hey, buddy! Hey!" the trucker shouted.

Roger sat up and glanced around. He knew he was back into his aching body on his way into the city, but the vivid dream left him with more questions.

Was this bizarre dream some sort of subconscious sign? he thought.

Roger was a man who didn't give much thought to his dreams. He never wrote down the strange images he had experienced, and figured the meaning of these visions was at a magnitude higher in the echelon of human life. Dreams, however, were important to Lois, and she would always write them down and discuss them with Roger over breakfast if something interesting filled her mind as she slept. When she was in the mood to write creatively, Lois always drew her inspiration from the visions that had touched her.

As Roger regained focus in the truck's cab, he wished he had a notepad to attempt to map the universe that had filled his dreaming mind, but as he looked around, the only object resembling paper was a mustard-stained parking ticket.

"Oh, I must have...dozed off," Roger finally responded.

"Don't worry about it. I didn't know if I should wake you, but we're coming into the city. Just passed the Pleasant Place Bridge. Did you hear about that bad accident last night? A few were killed from that tractor-trailer wreck. That driver must've been a pissin' idiot!"

News and current events were the last thing on Roger's mind. He knew he didn't have time to watch television or to read the paper. Those activities were part of a normal person's daily routine, not on the schedule of a man lost in his world. The bridge, however, jogged Roger's memory as he pondered his journey each day across the structure for work or for a date with his wife into the nightlife of the city.

"I'm surprised they had it open already. And you slept right through it," Jack said as he glanced into his side-view mirror.

Roger peered into the mirror on his passenger's side and saw the edge of the tall cables on the bridge. He wished he had seen the structure. The accident Jack explained piqued his attention, and he felt a desire to see the sight of this…accident.

Was my answer there? he thought.

"Say, what were you up to last night?" Jack added to his mostly one-sided conversation.

"I don't know. I'm trying to find my wife," Roger confided, but as he began to open up, Jack began to close down.

The trucker was the type who liked to toot his own horn, but when another fellow wanted to chime in, he just glazed over him. Jack focused on the busy city limits as a maze of green road signs reflected back at him.

"Hey, man. You got to do what you got to do. My turn is coming up here. I need to take the outer loop… How about I drop you in front of the mall?" Jack asked.

"Sure… I could really use something to eat," Roger responded.

Roger knew his ride's offer to assist was only a transport into the city and, now that they were there, the trucker's assistance had reached its end. Roger was anxious to explore the reason he had ventured to the heart of the city—the dinner reservation. While he didn't exactly know where to take his next step, being physically in the same area of his mind's last concrete image would hopefully lead to the next piece of the puzzle.

A shopping mall came into view on the side of the road as Jack gestured toward the gas stations, fast-food restaurants, and stores. While the sight of a gas station left a sour taste in Roger's mouth, a glowing hamburger establishment only sweetened it.

Jack turned into the large parking lot of the mall. As he calmed the bulldog he was driving, Jack glanced over to Roger's high-water pants. He chuckled to himself without letting it be known, but sincerely hoped his new friend would find his way. He reached into his jeans, grabbed a crumbled five-dollar bill, and then tossed it on Roger's lap.

"Go buy yourself something to eat. On me," Jack offered.

Roger exhaled as he prepared to respectfully refuse the kind gesture, but he didn't. He just grinned and looked at the burly man. Jack was his savior of sorts and no matter how he or his friends had looked down on blue-collar workers, sometimes the brawn of a sloppy truck driver was the best way to get back on one's feet.

"I appreciate everything, Jack. You're a good man."

"Hey. No problem. Just remember to watch out for those store displays!" Jack said.

"And alligators!" Roger added.

The truck stopped in the massive parking lot. Roger opened the clunky door and stepped down like an old man stepping out of a sedan. He splashed into a puddle of water left behind from a downpour and turned to look at Jack sitting high in his captain's chair. While Roger knew deep down that this was the first and last time he'd see his newfound friend, he would always think of Jack whenever he heard the roar of a tractor-trailer.

"Good luck!" Jack howled as Roger shut the door.

He stood in awe as the truck geared up and the engine came to life. The truck moved with grace, shifting in perfect rhythm. Roger thought how differently the truck looked from the outside, its black paint and dark windows giving it an enigmatic appearance. Roger, however, knew that even though it looked aggressive and menacing on the outside, compassion filled its heart. Then, like a card trick, the truck vanished in the shuffle of vehicles.

Roger felt the pain of hunger wrench his stomach. He faced the mall in the distance, but the deserted structure left him looking elsewhere to cure his appetite. Then like the family dog sniffing the neighbor's barbecue, Roger turned to the structure that tickled his senses, "Buddy Burger."

Roger moved toward the busy street with just four lanes separating him from food. The place was lit up under the starry sky as it tried to lure passing travelers by stimulating the sensitive rods in their eyes. Cars whizzed by in each direction and, for a moment, Roger felt like he couldn't make it across. Finally, he saw a break in traffic, but he paused for a second with the realization that his body might not make it. His hesitation transformed into panic, which made his breathing escalate and his heart race. Just as his heartbeat accelerated, a shot of adrenaline ignited him, which gave his steps enough pep to make it.

Large signs with promotional items were plastered on the all-glass facade. Cars scattered the small parking lot. Roger followed his sense of smell to the side of the building, and then to the entrance of the tasty edifice. A sign with a juicy hamburger caught his attention, "Get a Buddy Burger Deluxe and a Buddy-sized soda for only $3.99. Don't forget to bring your buddy!" While the cute wordage attempted to entice customers, this patron had no energy to be amused by a marketing gimmick. The picture of a mouthwatering burger magnified tens time to scale fixated him. He knew the pictures never resembled the actual item, but it didn't matter as only a glass door stood in the way of satisfying his hunger.

Roger pulled the handle to the door, but it failed to budge. At first, he questioned his misfiring muscles, but after a stronger tug, the door still mocked him. He looked through the cloudy glass spotted with dried rain and saw two male high-school aged workers. One was short and stout with a boyish face sporting a blotchy beard. The other was as thin as a rake and hunched over from his lankiness. They both wore silly shirts that were a piercing red color tarnished with grease stains. They swooshed mops back and forth on the floor. The two workers looked at Roger's image tugging at the door.

"Sorry, buddy, we're closed!" the short and stout worker yelled.

The lanky kid pointed at the clock on the wall. Roger tried to focus his eyes, which were overwhelmed by the bright interior lights, but as they adjusted, the minute hand, a smidge past nine o'clock, glared back at him.

"Come on, I'm starving here," Roger shouted through the glass barrier.

He looked at the workers and plastered the five-dollar bill on the door. If his image didn't allow entry, maybe Abraham Lincoln's would.

"Sorry...but our drive-thru is open," the lanky worker said, pointing.

Roger couldn't believe it. If he had arrived just a few minutes earlier, the doors would have been open. He thought about where he could have gained some time, crossing the street more quickly, less talk with Jack in the parking lot, or possibly even walking faster from the gas station to the trucker's vehicle. However, all of his thoughts were hindsight and the situation required him to roll with the punches, an all too familiar action.

The rear of the store was dimly lit with only the condensed menu illuminated behind the microphone.

119

Roger pondered his ability to order from the drive-thru. He had no idea where his black SUV was and, while he lacked a vehicle, he wondered whether one was actually required. His reasoning was if they couldn't discriminate against a handicapped individual, how could they discriminate against a man without a car? He referred to the group "they" as a collective body of society sliced to represent the overall cultural and political correctness of the time.

The moments of dithering mounted as he stood in front of the faceless microphone.

"Can I order a Buddy Burger?" he finally asked.

A void of silence replied. Then, the speaker emitted a loud buzz.

"Um... Uh, you can't order here," one of the kids said.

Roger squinted his eyes. For the first time he could recall, he felt discrimination—like a waitress failing to land a job based solely on her small cup size.

"Why not?" Roger barked back.

"Well, you have to order in a car. Sorry, we don't take walk ups."

"You've got to be kidding me!" Roger yelled.

He looked around to see if a covert camera was capturing his every movement, but he failed to locate such a device. He wanted a place to glare, a place to direct his rage. All he did, however, was throw his hands in the air in exhaustion. He was so close to satisfying his taste buds, yet a kid not even half his age was somehow given such authority. He glanced around and noticed a dumpster in the distance. For some reason, Roger gravitated toward it. Finding himself drawn to such an object baffled him; however, his primitive instincts had kicked in—the same instincts that drove the millions of bums who wandered the streets.

In the dumpster, Roger tossed around the refuse. He grabbed a folded newspaper, but threw it aside because a murky brown substance smothered its pages. Toward the bottom, a plastic bag was crumpled. Roger reached for it, trying to position the clear plastic in the hard overhead light. It housed a hundred hamburger buns, but as he rooted around inside, poisonous pieces of week-old bread scorned him.

Behind Roger, the headlights of a Buick sedan lurked around the building. Inside was an elderly couple out after a night of shopping. The elderly man drove around toward the rear of the hamburger joint ready to place his order. He craved a Buddy Burger with extra pickles and a side of fries, a snack he had frequently eaten after shopping at the mall across the street. His wife refused to eat after eight p.m., but she let her husband indulge after the shopping trip, which had been mainly for her. As they turned the corner, the headlights swept the dumpster. Light moved across the metallic bin and lit Roger just enough to reveal his desperation.

"Aww, that poor bum is searching for food," the elderly woman remarked.

"I wish they'd get a damn job!" growled her husband.

He was a man who gave a beggar on the street a word of advice instead of an ounce of loose change. This was because he had grown up on tomato sandwiches and sugar water, a childhood that had pushed him to work hard no matter what. The elderly man proceeded to order his meal as Roger, the wealthy man incognito, unearthed something to help him curb his hunger.

Moments later, the sound of squeaky wheels filled the cool night air. Roger sat on a beat-up red wagon like an eight-year-old mimicking the family sedan. In his mind, he thought his ploy would somehow work; after all, the definition of a vehicle was an ambiguous term. However, ambiguity was a word that most teenagers probably could not define, Roger concluded, and this simple fact would most likely stand in his way.

"I'd like to order now," Roger asked with a desperate tone.

Silence filled his ears, until finally the same teenager uttered, "Sir, you can't order unless you're in a car."

"I am! Define the word car," Roger whipped back.

"Well, uh, it has to be drivable."

"I can drive this just fine, you see," Roger explained as he moved the handle back and forth, figuring his demonstration would somehow vindicate his request.

"It has to have gas! You have to be able to fill it up!" the worker said.

Roger stood up and hurled the wagon in anger. He felt a tingle behind his ears, a sign that adrenaline was on its way through his body. "I don't believe this! I just want to order some food!"

Another vehicle approached the microphone. It was a bright red SUV about ten years old, but built to last, as its owner would brag. The man driving was a construction worker in his mid-fifties. He was trying to satisfy his appetite, which was building since his early lunch at eleven thirty. The driver noticed Roger rolling the red wagon back toward the dumpster.

The SUV stopped short of the microphone as its driver contemplated his order. Roger decided to try his luck at another approach. After all, he was a paying customer.

"Excuse me, sir. Can I ask a favor?" Roger said through the open passenger window.

The man turned and removed his focus from the menu.

"Um, what?" he stumbled.

"I don't have a car and I'm trying to order food. Well, um, I mean the dining room is closed and I don't have my car to order food in the drive-thru. Could I give you some money to order for me?" Roger said.

The man gave him a blank expression. He could understand how a beggar would do anything to stay alive, but he thought this man was different in that he actually offered money for his bizarre request. Luckily for Roger, the driver was someone who actually stopped and threw in some pocket change for the vagrant holding the cup at the traffic light.

"Uh, okay I guess," he responded.

Roger smiled, an expression that hurt his face. He reached into his pants pockets and dug around for the piece to his puzzle. Suddenly, he felt something metallic in his hand. He removed a set of car keys as both he and the driver furrowed their brows. Roger returned the item back into his pocket, the item he had unknowingly carried around since the hospital. Finally, he found the crumbled five-dollar bill and handed it to the driver.

What should I order? Roger thought.

Then the special plastered on the front of the door flashed in his mind, "Get a Buddy Burger Deluxe and a Buddy-sized soda for only $3.99. Don't forget to bring your buddy!" While Roger didn't bring his "buddy," he was sure the special didn't actually require proof of a friend's accompaniment.

"I'll just have a Buddy Burger Deluxe Special with a coke. Better make it a diet," Roger said.

The driver squinted. Here was a paying beggar who was concerned about his sugar intake.

Since most people in America seemed to be concerned with their diet, why shouldn't this apply to the bottom-class as well? the driver reasoned.

Roger found a place to camp out, behind a nearby utility shed, as the truck pulled forward to the awaiting microphone.

As Roger vanished into the night, the driver's ears filled with the squeal of the pubescent worker.

"Hi, welcome to Buddy Burger. May I help you?"

"Yes. I would like to order a number two combo, medium, with a coke."

"Is that everything?" responded the worker, ingrained with the overused question.

The driver looked down at the five-dollar bill as his eyes shifted to the deserted area. Even though he could not see Roger, he knew the man was awaiting his meal like a dog staring at its empty bowl.

"Sir?"

"No, that's not everything. I want an extra Buddy Burger Deluxe Special with a diet coke," he replied.

"Medium or large?"

He looked over and saw Roger emerge from the shadows.

"You'd better make it a large," the driver added.

"Okay. That will be eight seventy-one. Please pull ahead," the worker unemotionally responded.

The middle-aged man lifted his foot off the brake pedal. He looked toward Roger's location, but he was gone. The first window greeted the driver as he waited for the worker. After several moments, a figure appeared at the second window, waving the man forward. The short and stout worker revealed himself as the body that belonged to the voice. The worker sized up the SUV's driver, who suddenly felt nervous. The pimply faced worker, however, was totally detached from the moment.

His teenage mind wandered to the image of his female classmate's breasts and, as he offered the driver's change, his thoughts shifted to the same girl's legs. Then his accomplice, the lanky worker, slid toward the window and handed the man his bag of food. The smell of the cooked beef filled the cab of the truck as the man pulled forward, home free.

He drove into the last spot of the parking lot and parked his truck. He let the engine idle as he glanced around for his acquaintance. For a moment, he wondered whether the man actually swindled him, but after thinking some more, he realized he would not have been the victim of a ploy; it would have been the other way around. Roger finally emerged near the driver's side window.

"Here you go," the driver said as he handed Roger the burger and diet coke.

Roger widened his eyes. "Thank you, thank you. You don't know how hungry I am. Please, keep the change."

Again, his business instincts surfaced with his kind gesture, which baffled the construction worker.

"Hey. I don't need the change. I feel for you homeless out here," he responded as he handed Roger some coins.

Roger refused. His attention was completely focused on his hot, juicy burger. This was the cue for the driver to be on his way and, for a bizarre reason, he felt proud of his deed, even though he didn't exactly know what he had done.

I ordered this man some food with his own money, he thought, but he was happy to assist.

The SUV pulled away as Roger sat on the curb. Cars zipped by on the road in front of him as he unwrapped his meal. The warmth of the hamburger roused his cold fingers as he lifted the beef toward his mouth. His nose received a burst of Buddy Burger's special sauce just before he bit down. Then, the meat consumed the taste buds in his mouth.

"Aww, yes," he expelled.

The pain in Roger's arm and right leg subsided as he felt a sense of victory in his journey. It was as if another chapter in Roger's story had come to an end, but the remainder of his novel was far from complete.

14

The full moon pierced the night sky over the bustling city. As Roger satisfied his hunger, others focused their attention on finding the truth to the plight of the split couple. Det. Cleveland was on his way toward the sleeping beauty at Southern General Hospital. His trip back was similar to his drive in the opposite direction. However, he had the answer to his original question; Jane Doe was Lois Belkin. While this information was enough to solve the original case, it only answered part of the Belkin question—half in fact. He knew the location of Ms. Belkin, but Mr. Belkin was out wandering in the city building a rap sheet.

The glowing red "Emergency" sign burned into Det. Cleveland's eyes. He slowed to pull into the parking lot as he grabbed his cellular phone and dialed his proté-gé, Charlie, back at the fort.

He answered on the first ring as he kept the desk phone positioned between his keyboard and his late night snack, a double-decker Buddy Burger with extra pickles. He knew it was Det. Cleveland on the other line even before a spoken word. Charlie was a "fly on the wall" back at the station, something he had perfected, and he would use the "buzz" to enhance his research for Det. Cleveland.

"Yello?"

"Charlie, I know the identity of our Jane Doe. She is Lois Belkin from Dietrich Road. I need to ask a huge favor. Could you pull up any information on other family members of the Belkin's in the area?" Det. Cleveland rambled.

"Okay, where're you at, man?" Charlie replied, standing up.

"I'm at Southern General Hospital now. Get back to me Charlie as soon as you have any information.

Charlie sat down and leaned in to his desk.

"Okay, okay. No problem. Hey. You gotta get this Belkin before he causes any more trouble."

Charlie heard Roger's name mentioned at the dispatcher's desk about two hours ago after a call-in over the businessman's car debacle. Now that the patrolmen had returned from Roger's home with a report to the captain, Roger's name was moving up on the list of fugitive priorities.

Det. Cleveland paused, and then hung up the phone. He pulled his sedan into a spot marked "Police Parking Only."

As Det. Cleveland slammed his car door, a smaller and more compact door slammed across the city. It was Carol, another interested party thrown into the middle of her sister's case, but for her, she didn't know the brunt of the situation. The door she slammed was to the microwave oven as she popped in a TV dinner to satisfy a late-night craving.

Carol gave up on her voyage into the city, which turned her date with a baked black bean burrito into jury-duty with a three-cheese ravioli dinner frozen for nearly a year in the back of her freezer. Her husband, Robert, had phoned her about an hour ago and told her about a last minute overnight business trip to his company's sister office. She knew he probably had this planned for a while, and his decision to call her at the last minute was due to her unwillingness to let work overwhelm him. He stopped by to pick up an overnighter, which was suspiciously already packed, and gave her a kiss on his way out the door.

Her sole companion for the evening was her beagle, Lucy. The dog was often her only friend when Robert was away and her sister had plans. Lucy had a calm and docile temperament and never acted aggressively. After all, she was ten years old, which was nearly sixty in human years according to Carol's resources. She fed Lucy as soon as she got home from her unsuccessful trip into the city and now the lazy dog was basking in the warmth of the living room, letting her stomach do its work.

The beeps of the machine filled the kitchen, and then the device lit up and cooked her frozen dinner with its microwave radiation. Carol walked over to her kitchen window and looked out at the gloomy night. Clouds began to move in and steal the stars away. They moved quickly as one particular star caught her eye, and then, in a blink, a cloud choked the light from the distant luminary. A sudden feeling of loneliness overwhelmed Carol. For a moment, her lungs failed to respond to her breathing. It was a subtle feeling, but it was enough for her to turn and clutch her chest. She looked at a picture next to a magnet from Clearwater Beach on the refrigerator. Even though she was across the kitchen, the figures in the fuzzy four by six inch image were vividly clear. They were her sister and brother-in-law, Lois and Roger.

"I should call Lois," Carol told herself.

All was silent in the lifeless kitchen, save for the hum of the microwave. Carol walked over to the cordless phone and dialed Lois' number.

A few miles away through the shadowy night, the Belkin home stood dark and unconscious. Inside the master bedroom, the faint smell of Det. Cleveland's aftershave swirled in the open room, most noticeable in the attached bathroom. The moonlight shined through the bedroom's window, not yet victim to the encroaching clouds. On the nightstand was the picture of Lois and

Roger in front of the Hoover Dam. The light from the moon glimmered off the glossy photograph paper. In front of it, sat the bedroom phone, the same one Lois used when Carol had called the evening before. Tonight, however, was much different. Roger was not in the room putting the final additions on his suit. Lois was not in the bathroom making sure blush was symmetrical on both of her cheeks. Instead, a barren room echoed with the burst of the phone. As the rings went unanswered, the noise seemed to intensify.

On the other end, Carol repositioned the phone to her other ear. She was on the third ring and was hoping to hear a voice instead of her place in the phone system's black hole. Carol anxiously anticipated a click followed by Roger apologizing for being in the shower or Lois huffing after being preoccupied by a late night treadmill jog. However, none of these projected scenarios occurred.

The fifth ring echoed into her ear, and then the wave changed to a click. Carol stood on her heels, and for a moment she expected the voice of one of the two. Instead, she received the contrived voice of Roger.

Back in the deserted Belkin home, Roger's voice traversed through the open space, bouncing off the cold walls. "Hello, you've reached Roger and Lois. We're probably out and about, so please leave a brief message and we'll get back to you as soon as possible. Thanks."

A loud beep followed as Carol responded, "Hi, guys. I haven't heard from you since last night. Hope all is well."

Carol hung up the phone and crossed her arms to control the knot that had tightened in her stomach.

"Where could they be? I hope everything is alright," she whispered.

Carol pondered their location at this late hour. She looked at the clock. It was eight minutes after ten. Then, in a sudden burst, the beeps from the microwave stabbed Carol's sensitive ears; her hand dropped the phone.

15

The night air whirled through the downtown. Buildings stood tall under the overcast skies as late night cars zipped through the roads. People scurried through the night traversing the various bars and lounges. Some more elegant restaurants exhaled sophisticated couples as awaiting valet drivers sprang to action. An older husband and wife exited a swanky jazz club, "The Lookout House," and bypassed the valet service. Headed to a nearby public parking garage, they walked through the cool night air. As the elderly woman tightened her mink coat, she saw a figure approaching. It was Roger staggering toward them. Although he had given his belly something to work on, the pain in his right leg and arm returned. His previous painkiller, alcohol, wasn't in reach, and Roger was left alone to deal with the throbbing twinge hindering his journey. He didn't notice the approaching couple, but they noticed him.

The elderly woman hated walking the street at night. Even though her brazen husband had always held her tightly, she still dreaded the creatures lurking in the darkness. She and her husband saw what they classified as an approaching bum and realized he was not yielding to their steps. The woman slowed and stepped behind her husband so both could walk in single file. As they passed Roger, the elderly woman squeezed her husband's arm. Her nose received a blast of an unforgettable odor bellowing from Roger's battered body. She cringed. Roger kept focused on the concrete sidewalk and didn't even notice the couple. However, he glanced up after they had passed as he sniffed the woman's intense perfume.

Roger's sense of smell caused him to refocus on his surroundings. He looked up as he walked and noticed a brightly lit corner newsstand still open and eager to assist the night crowd. He saw magazines and newspapers from across the country, the world in fact, proudly displayed in rows to turn a wandering person into a staying customer. The man behind the register was the owner of the stand. He was fifty-two-years-old and took pride in his corner stand, so much so that he purposely worked the graveyard shift to protect his valuable assets. The owner was assisting a young lawyer pulling an all-nighter for an important case going to trial in the morning. He was buying some peanuts, caffeinated soda, and a copy of the latest men's magazine to arouse his sleep-deprived brain. Roger watched the lawyer reach into his trench coat and grab a leather wallet from the inside of his suit jacket. He studied the attorney's conforming leather gloves, the slight wrinkles of the material from the movement of his hand. Roger looked at the man as his mind refocused on the list of baffling questions. His brain felt confident declaring that he was in the city last night for dinner, but his exact intentions were still unknown. The most significant question still rang in his mind.

Where is she?

Roger held his head low and saw the front page of a newspaper. The headlines read, "Chaos on Pleasant Place Bridge." He looked at the prominent picture plastered on the front page, but as he tried to comprehend the image of terror, he heard the voice of the lawyer.

"Crazy, huh?" the attorney asked with disbelief. He looked at Roger's short pants and felt a hint of sympathy for the street dweller.

The image sank into Roger's mind as he made out the aerial view of the fiery mess on the bridge. He had never seen such a horrific image, and it almost appeared fabricated, like an image received in a dream.

"That tractor-trailer just annihilated those cars. Talk about being at the wrong place at the wrong time," the lawyer added.

Roger didn't know what his reference meant. The image in front of him showed specks of vehicles scattered on the bridge like the random placement by a boy dumping his matchbox cars on the ground. The lawyer grabbed another newspaper and tossed it in front of Roger, which explained the reference.

The paper highlighted images of scattered metal and auto parts, which resembled the remains of an auto graveyard. The tractor-trailer in the center of the image dominated the frame and towered above the helpless vehicles victim to its breadth. Roger glanced at the scattered auto parts. Suddenly, the whites of his eyes exposed as his mind received a flood of thoughts. It was as if the simple black and white image in front of him answered a chunk of his piling questions. However, the answers rapidly overwhelmed him. Then, he saw something gravely familiar in the picture. It was his black SUV crunched under the trailer of the truck. Roger could not speak; he could not listen; he could only be. All at once, half of the jigsaw board jolted into place.

I was involved in the accident, Roger's mind explained.

"I'd hate to be this guy," the lawyer rattled off.

Roger remained detached and aloof. The lawyer squinted, assuming Roger was being coy. Little did he know, however, that while Roger's body remained emotionless, his mind screamed with emotion.

"Hey, are you alright?" the lawyer asked.

Roger failed to respond. The lawyer shook his head and trudged off. He thought he was doing the bum a favor by indulging in conversation, but his one-sided chat only infuriated him.

A cool breeze whisked through and brushed the newspapers, causing them to crinkle in unison. Roger maintained focus on the image as the twinge in his body seemed to intensify. Then, his mind shifted to the thought of Lois. For a moment, he prepared to dart toward her rescue on the Pleasant Place Bridge, but he quickly recognized it was useless. Although he had slept through the passing on his journey into the city, Jack the trucker explained the bridge's reopening. Roger's black, late-model SUV was gone forever, but he hoped the fate of his wife was not the same. Roger yearned for her now more than ever.

"Lois, where are you?" Roger asked under his breath.

He used all of his energy to channel his thoughts to the aligning puzzle pieces. Suddenly, he found himself trapped in the middle of his vision. He felt like a puppet forced to follow his shell through the world of his distressed mind.

Roger was back driving his SUV. He glanced over and saw his wife in a killer black dress that contoured her curvy figure. The cruising V8 engine purred like a well-tamed lion. Up ahead, the Pleasant Place Bridge stood tall under the night sky. Then, in a burst, Roger's view filled with erupting flames. He heard screams of panic as he attempted to navigate through the fiery terror. His resistance was worthless as flames burst into the cabin. Lois suddenly became trapped. She cried for help. Roger tried to break his horrifying trance, but it was useless.

Suddenly, he heard a raspy voice, "Hey! You okay?"

Roger searched for the voice in his vision, but an inferno consumed his view. The voice returned, this time more prominent, "Yo, can you hear me?"

Roger snapped out of his coma. He blinked his eyes rapidly as the newspaper came back into focus.

"You alright there, mister? You don't look so good," the voice once again said.

Roger turned and saw a short male creature in his mid-thirties. He was barely five feet seven inches and had the face of a weasel, complete with the frail frame. Spots of food condiments splattered his ratty clothes. His hair was greasy and his teeth were yellow. The man was the type who even the rats avoided on the street.

Roger caught his breath from the abrupt sight, but the breath contained the rancid smell of perspiration infested with multiplying bacteria from weeks without a bath. He turned his head to acquire a fresh blast of night air. As Roger studied the beady-eyed man, he realized that his own appearance was not much different. While the adage explained, "opposites attract," Roger's luck with random strangers seemed to dwell on the lower echelon of society. The hobo reached out and patted Roger on the back. There was no way to ignore this prying person as he invaded Roger's space. Roger figured the best thing to do was to brush the weed off his back.

"I'm okay…just…confused," Roger replied while staring off at the traveling cars.

"You really should be careful out here. This city is dangerous at night," the critter quickly responded.

He extended his hand with a smile. The man's quick actions puzzled Roger, as his brain had no time to comprehend.

"Miles is the name, Miles Kay."

Roger looked away, but his cordial behavior ingrained from his professional career forced him to reach out.

Miles' hand was cold and felt rough like fine-grit sandpaper from years of living on the street. He was a man with a dark past, dropping out of high school, leaving an abusive home, and working odd jobs. This had been his life for years, and when he had finally exhausted the various fast food chains across the city, including Buddy Burger, the poorly educated man left for the streets. While he lacked book smarts, he made up for it with his wit and gut instincts. These kept him alive, and he used his survival tactics to keep his body fed enough so he would not starve like a homeless dog. While his outward appearance would make a paralyzed person run for his life, Roger somehow accepted him for…him.

"I'm Roger. I just had a rough day," he said.

Miles glanced at Roger's high pants. "Well, didn't we all. Where'd you come from? A flood?"

"It's a long story. I'm trying to figure out what happened yesterday."

Roger realized he had probably said too much. He usually asked the questions at the office prying for information from clients with his subtle tactics, but on the street things seemed to be backwards. Miles appeared to flip the tables and, after all, Roger was now a client in the street man's office. Roger turned and faltered away, hoping Miles would get the hint, but just as he stepped a few feet from his spot, Miles quickly followed.

"I'm forgetful too. I don't even know what day it is today. Ask me if I care. Go on," Miles insisted as he tugged Roger's shirt.

"I can tell you don't care. Yesterday…well, I'm trying to figure out where I was," Roger stuttered.

"Why? You on the run from somebody? Do you work for the government? Well, maybe I'm asking too many questions. Okay, I will help you. Just do what my daddy always says. God rest his soul. He was a good man. Died too young."

Roger had enough of the weasel. He shook his head and turned to walk away. This time, his steps were more prominent against the cold, hard concrete. The pain in his body suddenly subsided as the natural drug, adrenaline, flowed through his veins. Then in a flash, the leech lunged for Roger, this time using his body to block Roger's retreat.

"Whoa! Okay. Okay. I would say to retrace your steps. What did you do from when you got up till when you didn't remember? Then just go from there," Miles explained.

Roger looked across the street at a blind man walking the sidewalk led by a seeing-eye dog. He pondered Miles' advice and, while the short fellow didn't seem to know when to stop talking, he did make an ounce of sense with his comment.

"Well, that's actually a good idea," Roger said as he focused on the dog looking both ways before guiding the man across the street.

"I told you my daddy was a smart man," Miles added.

"I remember coming home from work, then seeing my wife," Roger explained, scratching his head.

"Then?"

The vivid black and white images in the newspapers clouded Roger's progression through his memory, but he did his best to keep his train of thought on track. He remembered the reason he gravitated to the city in the first place, the reason he trekked down the road, hitched a ride from a shameless trucker, and even fought to curb his hunger.

"I remember going to eat somewhere downtown," he continued.

Abruptly, his mind hit a wall of fire. Roger watched as the blind man walked toward them. He was tall and wore a dark trench coat with his face covered with dark glasses, making him look out-of-place for a walk at night. The furry Labrador leading the way turned Roger's gawks of bafflement into stares of empathy. The dog reached the two street dwellers dithering on the sidewalk and sniffed Roger's ankle. As he felt the dog's breath, the animal licked Roger's exposed skin. Roger did not pull away from the dog's warm tongue as his energy diverted to the skin of his ankle. Then the blind man passed on his way, unaware of the dog's diversion. Suddenly, it happened, a moment of clarity. Roger looked at the bright city lights with a piece of knowledge he had so desperately sought.

"Yeah, that's right. The Hideaway on Fourth Street. I need to get over there," he said as he perked up.

"Hey. That's a good idea. But Fourth Street? That's a walk to China on foot," Miles said.

Roger knew it was several miles from his spot, but he didn't care. He began to walk toward the heart of the city where the next leg of his journey awaited. Miles, like a lost child, followed Roger's lead, but then the lost businessman stopped abruptly.

"Whoa, where are *you* going?" Roger asked.

Miles licked his lips as he confided in Roger. "Hey. I wanna help you. These streets can get pretty scary at night. I know them like the back of my hand. My daddy always said help a man on a mission. Or was it beware of a man on a mission?"

"What do you want out of this? Huh?" Roger barked. He knew to be wary of people who talked fast as they usually tried to mask their agenda in words battering your ears like a prizefighter.

"Nothing, honest. Hey. I don't have much to do. I usually just roam the streets. I don't really have a place to live. I was staying in some guy's car up there on the north side. It didn't have a driver's side door though, so it was kinda breezy at night," Miles explained.

He looked at Roger as a person he could help, a fellow drifter with an actual purpose. Miles was being sincere when he explained his typical day. Most of the time he lived without a purpose, a feeling that was best left to the dead. He had no place to be, no errands to run, no clock to watch. The proverb asked the question whether a tree that fell in the woods made a noise if no one was there to listen to it. Miles asked himself a similar question every day, "If a bum screams before he dies on the streets, has he influenced the world in some way if no one stops to listen?"

Roger studied him and saw a twitch to his right eyelid. Although his fast-talking took some time to digest, Roger realized the man did have some interesting insight into solving his problem.

The observation from a third party may actually hold some value, he thought.

"Okay, okay," Roger finally replied.

Like a child getting clearance to go out and play, Miles smiled and stood next to Roger. Both men trudged down the sidewalk on their long walk through the night. Clouds enwrapped the city and stole the starry sky, but Roger didn't need the stars for direction. He knew exactly where he had to go, a place that he hoped would hold the answer to the ultimate question—where is Lois?

16

The color blue filled the nurses' station on the recovery floor of Southern General Hospital. It wasn't the metaphoric color, but the literal color of the nurses' standard issue scrubs. The hospital employed more staff nurses during the overnight hours than at any other time of the day. Their logic was that the night brought in more patients, victim to the enigma of night. Statistically, there were more car accidents, more alcohol-related injuries, and more crimes that involved violence. Something about the absence of light incited the need for medical attention and Southern General made sure the hospital was staffed accordingly. This was particularly true of the recovery floor as they received the brunt of the patients making it out of the emergency room.

There were five nurses on staff during the grave-yard shift, plus a supervisor. All were female, not because of any employment prejudice, but simply because eighty percent of the hospital's nurses were female. With this high percentage, a grouping of five females was statistically more likely. The nurses liked working the night shift on the recovery floor for the sole reason that they regarded their supervisor, Nurse Ann, as an important role model, mentor, and friend.

Things were quiet as the nurses filled out patient logs, prepared nightly drug dosages, and monitored the patients' call buttons. Across from the nurses' station stood a bank of elevators reflecting the light from their polished metal. Disrupting the quiet, a ding sounded. A dainty freshman nurse, Jennifer, sat directly in front of the elevators. She was compiling a list of doctors' notes from the rounds of the day as she looked up anticipating the elevator's occupant. Since it was past visitation hours, she figured the elevator housed one of the creepy janitors who enjoyed flirting with the nurses who fell into the eighty percent category. The doors opened as the nurse's eyes focused on the ground. She expected to see a mop bucket, but instead she saw a pair of gleaming male dress shoes. Her eyes widened as they traveled up and saw pressed dress slacks and a dapper trench coat. Finally, her eyes landed on the handsome face of Det. Cleveland. He had a hint of stubble painting his defined face, which tickled the female nurse's senses. She saw him sway toward her in slow motion as his alluring eyes locked with hers. The other female nurses glanced over and watched the arresting detective glide with confidence. He stopped in front of the freshman nurse and grinned.

"Hi there," Det. Cleveland said.

His masculine voice flowed through her as she felt her nipples harden.

"Hello," Jennifer replied with a smile.

"I'm looking for Nurse Ann."

Nurse Ann stood in the back office organizing the nurses' schedule for the coming week. She had heard the ding of the elevator and assumed that it was one of the peculiar janitors, but as she glanced at her staff, she knew that it wasn't one of the grubby men. She saw all of the women staring in the same direction like sophomores eyeing the senior quarterback. Nurse Ann beheld the cool Det. Cleveland standing tall in front of the counter. Immediately, she sprang to his attention.

"There she is," he said with a smile to the freshman nurse.

Nurse Ann walked around and met Det. Cleveland on the other side. She noticed he had a glimmer in his eye that was not present before.

"Hi. I've got good news," he continued.

Nurse Ann lifted her heels off the ground.

"Our Jane Doe. Her name is Lois Belkin. She and her husband Roger were in an SUV which took the brunt of the damage in the crash."

His words dropped her feet down to the cold floor. His seemingly simple explanation was loaded with life-changing events that took some digesting. She raised her hand to her mouth and inhaled.

"Oh, God. How did you find this out?" her voice expelled through the space between her fingers.

"Well, that's what they pay me to do. I have my department looking for any relatives."

Nurse Ann thought finding the answer to her burning question, Jane Doe's identity, would provide some closure in the case. After all, the patient no longer was the mystery woman lying in the secluded room. However, naming her did the opposite; it opened up a book of new and more daunting questions. She thought about the name Lois Belkin and how many of her family members were devastated over her absence. Nurse Ann leaned her back against the wall as she took a moment to collect her thoughts. She reviewed the detective's words and repeated them over and over again in her mind. Floating to the top, a question dominated her thoughts.

"What about her husband...Roger?"

As she spoke his name, she realized that Roger might actually be a patient of hers. The name didn't sound familiar, but Jennifer at the floor's computer could check the database.

"Jen, can you look to see if we have a Roger Belkin?"

Before anyone could act, Det. Cleveland interjected. "He's not here. He was admitted to Saint Peters

North Hospital, but unexpectedly checked himself out. He suffered some bad head trauma, and he's been doing some strange things around the city. We're trying to track him down."

"Oh, dear," Nurse Ann let out. She felt a strange feeling of remorse overwhelm her. The thought of the man wandering the streets in search of his wife hit her harder than a truck in a car wreck. She knew that Saint Peters North Hospital was more than ten miles away across the breadth of the city. Nurse Ann pondered Det. Cleveland's choice of words in describing Roger Belkin and his actions, namely the word "strange." She knew head trauma was a menacing handicap. The mind was a powerful object when used to its potential with the ability to function, to reason, and to understand the very essence of life. It stored our memories, collected our thoughts, and provided a myriad of functions that defined our unique being. The mind, however, provided life a disservice when a devastating injury had afflicted it. Unlike a broken bone or laceration, the mind's damage had no concrete healing pattern. A seemingly innocuous image or idea could trigger an amplification of the injury or mend the damage altogether. With this stark truth, Nurse Ann hoped she could help Roger.

"Is he in trouble?" she asked.

Det. Cleveland remained mute. She knew his silence was a nice way of saying "yes."

"How is Lois doing?" he finally asked.

Nurse Ann's focus returned to the unconscious woman down the hall. Det. Cleveland's question was something she could answer and the best way she figured to reply was to bring the man to her room. Nurse Ann gestured for him to follow her. As she walked, she realized something powerful from his simple, four-word query. It was something that was not outwardly present and even the eavesdropping nurses hadn't recognized it. It was the fact that Det. Cleveland used the word "Lois" to describe the unconscious patient. He didn't refer to her as the "subject" or the "woman." He acknowledged her as a living and breathing human being with a name, and his question showed a chink in his otherwise impenetrable emotional armor.

The duo walked down the dimly lit west wing of the recovery floor. The hospital lowered the light output on its floors after ten o'clock in order to save energy and to provide a more tranquil setting for the less traveled floors. It took Det. Cleveland's eyes a moment to adjust. His footsteps echoed off the hard floors, but as Nurse Ann stopped near the door to Lois' room, he could make out the heartbeat monitor through the thick oak.

Nurse Ann pushed open the door as the cool air tickled Det. Cleveland's nostrils. Both softly slid into the room. Det. Cleveland studied Lois. The sheets covered her petite body perfectly and were folded down just above her chest. Her breaths were rhythmic and slower than the electronic beats. Her left arm rested on her stomach, and her fingers were slightly curled. A white cast propped up by a sling wrapped Lois' right arm. Det. Cleveland looked at her emotionless face resting like a pure and innocent baby. She was much more beautiful than he remembered in the photograph at the Belkin home. This was the "dynamite" in Roger's life, and her current presence was quite the opposite than the literal meaning of the noun. This woman added life to the house that Det. Cleveland had analyzed earlier that night, but just as her house lie dormant, so did Lois Belkin.

"Well, unfortunately, her condition is unchanged. She is stabilized. Her arm was set and should heal correctly. The coma is her only obstacle now," Nurse Ann explained as she placed her warm hand on Lois' cheek.

Det. Cleveland felt his stomach clench as he thought of Roger lost on his voyage.

"I hope she—" he began to say, but his phone cut him off before he could finish the sentence. "Excuse me," he said as he stepped into the hallway.

The door shut behind him.

"Hello?"

"Hey, Ray. Bad news," Charlie said.

Det. Cleveland swallowed, nervous about his right hand man's loaded response.

"Well, I haven't been able to pull up any info on our Jane…er Lois Belkin. Our database has no other Belkins in the county. But if she was treated like a missing person, we could probably get more visibility with the media," Charlie explained.

Det. Cleveland licked his lips. He was surprised by Charlie's suggestion. This was the perfect example of a moment where his protégé stepped up and rolled with the punches. While Lois was not a missing person, following the same channels would open up new possibilities of finding one of her family members. The ultimate outcome would be to locate the most important relative, her husband.

"Let's get her face out there. Put it out on the news wire and attach a story looking for next of kin. Have any callers contact the watch down at the station," Det. Cleveland directed.

"Check," Charlie replied.

He was glad Det. Cleveland agreed with his clever suggestion. The easy part of his conversation was over as Charlie leaned deep into the towering papers on his desk for privacy.

"Hey, by the way, her husband Roger is really digging himself a grave. He was spotted at a gas station skipping out from paying. He was with some trucker headed toward the downtown. I don't know what this guy is planning, but the front line down here is getting pretty uneasy. The captain wants him picked up ASAP," Charlie whispered.

"Don't worry about him, I got it covered."

"I don't know if that's what the captain—"

"I don't give a damn what the captain wants! I was assigned to the Jane Doe case and now we know her name is Lois Belkin. But I need to talk to her husband to close this all out. I will take care of it!"

Charlie held the phone away from his ear to lessen the punch. He was trying to be diplomatic with the detective, but Charlie knew when to stop and accept Det. Cleveland's guidance.

"Okay, but just know the front line has him on their radar," Charlie added.

"Charlie, please just patch any updates to me personally. I could really use your help on this," the detective responded as he slammed his cell phone closed.

Det. Cleveland took a moment to digest his conversation with Charlie and realized his right hand man was just doing his job of relaying information. His anger was really focused on the belligerent captain and the front line of first responders who were more like puppets than a free-thinking force. None of them experienced the direct knowledge of the Belkin family, split apart by the destructive accident. The detective was given privileged information into the lives of this divided couple and, with this information, he had a duty to serve and protect.

Det. Cleveland turned and looked at Lois through the small glass window. Nurse Ann was sitting on a chair near her side and was softly stroking her hair like a mother cuddling her sleeping child. The sight made him grin with contentment, as he had finally named the woman lying through the door. The larger and more pressing piece of the puzzle, however, transcended the room in front of him. It rested somewhere outside in the darkness of night. The man who shared the photograph with Lois was lost in his own world, a world contorted into something unthinkable.

"Roger, where are you?" Det. Cleveland murmured.

He realized he had no strong leads in finding the lost man. His only crutch now was logic, and it told him to trace the known course of the unknown traveler. Det. Cleveland looked around and understood what he needed in order to begin his search—a city map.

As the detective marched to the facility's engineer to track down his city's guide, the lobby of Southern General Hospital was surprisingly busy for the clock passing eleven p.m. A janitor sloshed a mop back and forth in front of an information desk staffed with two college interns. Although the administrative functions were sparse at this hour, the doctors and nurses assigned to the emergency room flurried with activity. Just like the nursing staff, the hospital employed more doctors during the graveyard shift than at any other time of the day due to the increase in emergency related admissions. The lobby was the central hub for the pathway between the emergency room and the cafeteria, which explained the bustle of activity.

The elevator bank in the back of the lobby stood closed as most of the activity revolved around the main floor. Then, a ding sounded, breaking the silence. The door opened as Det. Cleveland walked toward the main hospital doors. A city map was rolled under his arm marked with a search plan to cover the potential pathways Roger could be traveling. They included the assumption of Roger's journey on foot, but the detective realized that hitching a ride was a real possibility and could yield a much larger search radius. Either way, Det. Cleveland knew what he had to do.

As he looked at the automatic sliding doors, they suddenly opened, triggered by two moving bodies on the other side. Det. Cleveland expected to see white lab coats or an ambulance driver strolling inside, but he saw the badges of two individuals dressed in black, standard-issue uniforms. Even though he was several yards away, he recognized the distinct shape of the badges. They were issued by one, and only one, specific entity—the city police department. After determining their origin, the detective looked up at their faces, and then squinted his eyes in thought. Both looked bizarrely familiar not because they were cops, but because he had met the two recently. One was a scrawny man with oversized clothes who was sporting a trite mustache on his boyish face. The other was a husky individual with a plump belly that probably held his stash of donuts. They were the two officers mucking around earlier in the night in the Belkin's liquor cabinet. Both had coy expressions and, as Det. Cleveland neared them, they obviously were clowning around…again.

"Hey, guys. What's going on?" Det. Cleveland asked as both stopped and straightened up.

"Oh, hi, sir. We're on our way upstairs. The captain wants a stake-out on the Jane Doe," the burly patrolman said.

Det. Cleveland's expression remained emotionless, but his blood was boiling. He knew the captain had the wrong idea of Roger; thinking the man was a threat to anyone was outrageous. Det. Cleveland was on top of the situation, but as he was a man who separated himself from the mainstream, so did his superiors. He was outraged that the captain had required a stake-out for Lois' room, and it was even more appalling that he sent two fools, no less, to perform the task.

"Her name is Lois Belkin," Det. Cleveland responded.

"Sorry, yes. Well, we're here just in case hubby Belkin shows up. He's been upgraded on our priority list," the hefty patrolman replied.

"Grand Theft Auto. Retail Theft. Evading Arrest," his skinny counterpart listed.

Det. Cleveland couldn't believe what he heard. These nitwits were actually serious with thinking this man, this victim, this husband, was actually an evil outlaw preying in the city. While on paper these crimes were indeed flagrant, a simple glance at the complete details of the situation would prove the series of events as circumstantial and unfortunate. Det. Cleveland was surprised at his own compassion for the case; in the past, he would have sided with the by-the-book captain, but this case was different. He was somehow given the privilege to see into the lives of Roger and Lois Belkin, to understand them, to empathize with them. It was ironic, however, that he had never actually met either of them, but that didn't hamper the conviction he had for doing the right thing.

Both patrolmen snickered from the laundry list of Roger's offenses, which only added to Det. Cleveland's disgust.

"So, we'll be upstairs baby-sitting," the burly patrolman chuckled. He turned to his comrade. "Why do we always get the shit jobs?"

"No. Why do *you* always get the shit jobs?" the scrawny man replied.

Both men resembled schoolboys clowning around when they should have been focusing on work. The main difference between schoolboys and patrolmen was that the latter carried a weapon, which made clowning around a deadly game.

Det. Cleveland had enough. "Hey, well just don't go jerking around up there! And keep me up to date if you see any sign of Mr. Belkin."

Both patrolmen jolted from Det. Cleveland's burst of energy. Both felt intimidated by his commands, the scrawny one in particular, but the burly patrolman thought of his conversation with the captain. It was actually more like a lecture by the potent man and, while Det. Cleveland and the captain were both above him in rank, the higher positioned always trumped when orders barked. The captain's boisterous voice still rattled inside his head, "I want this Belkin now!"

"Well, we have specific orders to only go through the captain's office," the husky patrolman responded.

"I don't believe this! Just don't go playing Robocop!" Det. Cleveland yelled as he stared at the door. He knew he was up against the wall on this one; he was now a lion isolated from the pack, a position that required killer instinct and determination to survive.

Det. Cleveland charged past the two patrolmen toward the door. At this point, the whole lobby focused their attention on the detective. The interns behind the information desk were wide awake from their normally dismal night, and the janitor stopped his work to watch the striking man march with conviction. He thought to himself, *Now that looks like a man on a mission.*

17

The late night streets bustled with the cocktail crowd. It was nearing "last call" at the city's bars and restaurants, but that didn't stop the night dwellers from overindulging. One of the hopping places under the cloudy sky was The Hideaway. The cool breeze picked up to a chilly wind, but none of the extravagant patrons leaving the restaurant seemed to care. They simply tightened their overcoats and buttoned their animal furs as the valet drivers scurried to retrieve their vehicles.

Roger and Miles stood across the street peering at the building like two wannabe robbers casing a jewelry store. They had walked over two miles through the dark streets, but finally made it. Roger watched as a gray-haired man in a trench coat handed a young valet driver his ticket, which prompted the youth to hustle toward the side garage. For a brief moment, Roger pictured himself as that man. While it was several hours later than a date for him and Lois, an eerie feeling of déjà vu tingled his subconscious senses. As his thoughts swirled, the valet driver returned with a white SUV. Roger widened his eyes as the valet driver commanded a bizarrely similar make and model. At first, Roger doubted the vehicle as an exact replica, save for the pure color, but the large silver-finished rims shined in such a way that confirmed the vehicle's exactness. Roger could not talk. He could only watch as the valet driver opened the door for the elegant woman accompanying the man. Roger could not see her face. He tried to reposition his neck, but the pain in his muscles nagged him.

Is that Lois?

Somehow, he couldn't be sure unless he saw her face. The woman entered as the tinted glass consumed her identity. Then, the man in the trench coat walked around the side and handed the valet driver some money. The young worker opened the driver's side door and the gap gave Roger a moment of direct view of the woman. She was much younger than the man, about thirty, and she had a softness to her feminine features. The woman glanced up and, for a brief moment lasting less than a second, her eyes connected with Roger's. It was as if she knew he were there watching from across the street. Roger wondered whether she was placed in front of him for a reason, a subtle signal to confirm his presence just over twenty-four hours ago. The SUV's engine roared down the road into the night. Suddenly, Miles' nasally voice filled Roger's ears as he jarred from his own universe back into reality.

"Hey, is that the place or what?"

"Yeah, that's the place. I was there last night," Roger said.

"Ha-ha, I bet you were. I myself was having broiled lobster with the Queen," Miles boasted.

Roger thought about responding with the pieces of the puzzle he knew in his mind, waking up in a hospital, journeying from his house to the city, or how the SUV he just watched drive away resembled his black SUV demolished in the crash on the bridge. He needed to transfer the vivid images traversing his mind to Miles like uploading information over a computer network. Roger, however, could not do that; he could only use words to communicate. Since talk was cheap, in fact it was free, he had no way and no desire to explain the events gusting through his mind. Roger decided to use his energy to move forward, instead of to dwell in the past. Besides, the runt following him was getting on his already stressed nerves.

"The Queen? What? Were you in London?" Roger lashed back, trying to defuse Miles.

"The Queen, I like to refer to our mayor as the Queen," Miles responded.

"But our mayor is a man," Roger replied shaking his head.

He realized it was useless to provide any clarity to the weasel's illogical logic. What was logical, however, was another clue to his riddle just across the street. An image flashed into his mind. It was of a burly fellow holding two wine glasses. Then, a bell rang. It was his waiter from last night.

"I need to talk to our waiter. John, I think. He might be able to fill in the gap after dinner," Roger continued.

"Okay, I got ya. So we need to talk to John. What if he's not working?" Miles said.

"I don't know. I have to at least check. It's my only clue."

Roger checked for an opening in traffic. He knew his fatigued muscles required extra time to function. A car passed as Roger saw headlights several blocks away. A window of opportunity presented itself. Roger took it and scuttled across the street. Miles followed, mimicking the moves of his mate. Roger saw the door to the restaurant a half block in front of him. Valet drivers swarmed the front like the Queen's Guard defending Buckingham Palace. He paused to contemplate the best line of attack, but then Miles walked into his back.

I have to get rid of this guy, he thought.

It was one thing to take advice from a man with an intimate connection with the streets, but a drifter was someone Roger had no interest in befriending. He wondered if Miles' persistence was due to a genuine interest in his mission or if it were just for his own personal amusement. Either way, Roger was putting his foot down, even if his foot had pained him.

"I'm going to go in alone. I don't want them to think we're staying," Roger said with conviction.

"You sure? I could distract them while you—"

"We're not robbing the place! Just give me a few minutes."

He pushed Miles away, trying to get his response embedded into the stubborn man's brain. In his thirty-five years, Roger couldn't remember actually resorting to violence to seal a deal. His urge surprised him, but then again, so did every other action he had performed this day. He was a fish out of water, but he would fight his way through an army on the streets to find the woman who made his heart beat.

Miles became quiet. His eyes stared at the ground. Roger's jolt seemed to add the right punch to where his words faltered, which made him proud. He hoped Miles would listen to his commands, as he wanted to focus his energy on solving his conundrum, not on managing a mutt.

Roger slithered toward the entrance. He knew his outward appearance would certainly create a ruckus with the gatekeepers, so he slowed in anticipation of a diversion. The door came closer, but a distraction failed to surface. No one walked from the front of the restaurant, which would spring the awaiting dogs to fetch a bone. As Roger panicked, a high-class couple exited the building prompting the two valet drivers to butt heads to assist the patrons. The opportunity presented itself. Roger picked up his steps, but the pain in his leg intensified. Now was not the time to waver. Roger scrunched his brow in an attempt to manage the pain.

"Thank you, sir. It'll be one moment," the valet driver responded to his customer.

The glass door was a few more steps away. Roger eyed the glass, which reflected the image of his potential captors. Suddenly in the reflection, Roger saw a hefty valet driver reaching toward him. He prepared to be seized and tossed down, but quickly realized the distorted perspective made the valet driver appear closer than he actually was. The valet driver, in fact, was reaching toward the well-dressed man waiting for his vehicle. He was a tax accountant and offered the valet driver his business card, a typical action he performed to promote his private company. Roger reached for the door handle and felt the cool metal on his sweating palm. He pulled it and scurried inside, but then realized the small hurdle to enter the building was only the beginning as he found himself inside a lion's den.

The shadowy interior engulfed Roger's senses as his eyes took in the wide angle. He smelled an intoxicating perfume, and his ears focused on the sound of laughing. The concoction of his new environment caused him to stop cold, trying to process the location. One side led toward the deserted hotel lobby, while the other opened up to the unique restaurant. Roger forgot the intention of his arrival into the building, but then he realized it was the search for a server named John. His eyes fully adjusted, as he looked to his left. Abruptly, he jumped back as he saw a horrifying image, an image of pain, an image of darkness. Little did Roger know, the image was not from this world, but created with brushstrokes of paint on canvas. The face of the shrieking man in Munch's *The Scream* glared at Roger. He finally realized it was just a painting on the wall.

The laughing continued, which turned Roger's focus. Off in the distance, he saw a woman across from a smiling man at a table in the restaurant. The placid place settings added a certain finesse to the dinner tables with other classy couples sprinkling the area. Roger raised his head, flaring his nostrils to find the feminine perfume. He finally saw its owner. It was the cute hostess behind the nearby podium.

Roger shuffled toward the young woman. She was the same bubbly hostess from his previous encounter working a double shift tonight, but Roger couldn't place her. As he neared the young woman, however, he realized her bizarre familiarity. It wasn't her face; it was her cleavage. Roger stared at her chest as a flash of his encounter with her flowed through his mind. He remembered the bubbly girl seating him and Lois last night. While the environment mimicked his experience from the night before, one crucial detail was missing. Roger looked to his left, but a void filled the space once occupied by his love. Finally, he returned to reality as he shifted his eyes to the face of the hostess, but the expression she had was no longer warm and vivacious. She darted her eyes around the room, as if in search of something. She had no smile, and she nervously flicked her ear as she squirmed in place.

"Um, can I, uh, help you?" she asked without making eye contact.

"I was looking for a server. I think his name is John," Roger asked.

"Um, what?"

"A server. Is John working tonight?"

Nearby, the stout manager from the previous night walked around the corner. He had been in the kitchen putting out a stove fire, but when the cooks had it under control, he decided to focus his attention on offering thanks to the departing patrons. As he rounded the corner to the entryway, he saw Roger hovering over the innocent hostess. The manager widened his eyes and picked up his steps, as he wondered how another bum had breached the front line of defense.

"Hey, is everything okay here, April?" the manger interjected.

"Oh, I was looking for John," Roger replied as he turned toward the baritone voice.

The manager cut through the tension and inserted himself between beauty and the wandering beast. The manager took the opposite approach with Roger and instead of failing to maintain eye contact, he stared back with a look of rage.

"I'm going to have to ask you to leave," he snarled.

"I don't understand," Roger innocently replied.

As the pressure intensified, a burst of noise erupted from the door behind Roger. Everyone instinctively turned toward the commotion, including most of the patrons. It was Miles pouring through the door like a spoiled carton of milk spilling on the freshly polished kitchen floor.

"Hey, Roger, did you find him? Is this him?" Miles yelled.

"Get out of here you two!" the manager commanded.

Roger couldn't believe Miles' disruption. He knew he should have tied down the weasel.

"I don't understand the problem. I was here last night," Roger continued.

However, it was too late. The manager had enough of the commotion. Several couples gasped from the disorder. A middle-aged woman having a drink with her husband rolled her eyes and scorned the bums, as she classified them.

Two muscular servers sprang to action as the manager signaled to them. This was the second night in a row that bums had entered his establishment, which made his temper flare. He was not going to let these two disrupt his customers.

"You're trespassing on private property. I'm going to call the police if you don't leave here immediately," the manager snarled.

Miles tried to resist the encroaching server as the manager jumped toward the phone. Finally, one of the servers grabbed Miles and dragged him toward the door.

"Hey, get your meat hooks off me!" Miles shouted.

A female server dropped her tray of drinks as the chaos surprised her. Glasses shattered. Another woman screeched.

Roger positioned his neck to see if he could make out John through the confusion, but he soon found the other server's hands grasping his shoulder. Roger conceded as the man ejected him out the door.

Outside the restaurant, Miles and Roger spewed from the glass doors and hit the concrete like rag dolls. The two servers towered over them and wiped their hands clean.

"And stay out! We don't cater to bums," the server manhandling Miles exclaimed.

"Get out of here!" Roger's bully belted to motivate the two away from their establishment.

A prudish old woman walking nearby looked down at the action and shrieked. She clutched her husband's arm as The Hideaway's finest worked on Roger and Miles.

The valet drivers gathered around the two and formed a circle with the only open part toward the south end of the sidewalk.

Roger rolled around on the hard pavement. He felt his bones yell. Since Miles was closer to the ground and frequently used the earth as his own bed, he had suffered a lesser impact. Therefore, his bones had accepted the fall with more ease, and while it certainly hadn't been like one performing a dive onto a comfortable bed, it had been graceful compared to Roger's tumble.

Miles picked up Roger and hustled down the sidewalk as the gang of men roared at them.

"I can't believe those clowns. The nerve!" Miles said.

"Let's get out of here before the cops come," Roger replied.

"Yeah, me and the fuzz don't mix."

Roger knew how the police seemed to have the wrong idea of his intentions, but the cards he played all ended in a bust.

Miles seemed to have a spark in his step that Roger lacked. He led the way on the sidewalk as the two headed toward the cross street. Miles turned the corner ahead of Roger and, for a brief moment, the lost businessman felt a sudden feeling of emptiness. Then, however, an image stopped him cold. He realized he was not alone as the pristine glass store reflected his true self. The man in the mirror startled Roger. While the tousled hair and grubby clothes looked the same as his previous meeting with the man, blood, scuffs, and bruises now painted his face and neck. The reflecting wanderer seemed to be spiraling downhill. While their meetings focused Roger's attention and gave him a look into his new universe, he feared his next encounter with the reflection.

"Where're you at?" Miles asked from around the corner.

He peered around and saw Roger entranced in the window of the closed business. He looked up at the unlit sign and saw "Frankie's Dry Cleaning." Miles wondered why Roger was interested in getting his clothes dry cleaned, but figured his shirt and pants did need a good scrubbing.

Maybe they could let out the cuffs in his pants to add a few more inches, he thought.

Miles' voice brought Roger out of his fixation. Then in a flash, the visitor in the glass vanished into the emptiness of the night. Roger continued down the sidewalk behind his leader, but his brief moment of reflection left him feeling overwhelmed with his journey. He was so close to finding a clue to his mystery, but as he trekked farther from The Hideaway, he felt far away from the woman he loved. Roger looked ahead and saw a mess of identical streets with no clear direction in sight.

18

The night grew even darker as thick clouds overwhelmed the moonless sky. The humidity level had increased. Water vapor whirled with the gusts of wind whipping through the city skyscrapers. Roger sat on the sidewalk curb with his legs extended as cars sporadically sped by. He felt clobbered, beyond the breaking point of a tree branch used as a crutch. He put all of his eggs in one basket marked The Hideaway, but all of those eggs had been thrown onto the street and smashed to unsalvageable pieces.

Miles sat next to Roger with a look of defeat covering his dirty face. He was with Roger one hundred percent on his journey, bonded with him by the unwritten code of the street. It was the same relationship as bikers who would give a friendly wave to a passing motorcycle or veterans who would watch each other's back even on the first meeting. Miles liked Roger not only because he was a fellow drifter, but also because he had a concrete goal in mind. It was a goal that Miles didn't fully understand, but he admired the way Roger focused his attention on the next obstacle in his path.

Roger had no more energy to continue. A void filled his mind. It was a feeling of sheer nothingness, and he sensed the end was near. He stared with an expressionless face, mouth gaping an inch, at a pothole in the street. He watched the tires of each car as they drove over the hole with their force chipping more and more of the tarred road away and widening the infection. Roger wondered how the insignificant hole would fair against the girth of a fully loaded tractor-trailer. For a bizarre reason he felt connected to the hole, understanding its pain of constant abuse. Roger wished the hole were bigger so he could lie inside and receive the fate that he had cheated on the bridge.

"I don't believe that guy at the restaurant," Miles said in his chipper tone.

Miles picked up a stone and threw it into the hole in a perfect shot. The rock jarred Roger's fixation on the pothole.

"I mean, we didn't even see your waiter friend," Miles replied as he threw another stone.

This time it missed the hole and skipped across the street. "I'm hungry. Wanna get some fast food?"

Miles' nasally voice struck a chord in Roger's eardrum. He looked at the man sitting next to him, always tooting his horn. Then it hit him. Roger realized it was this pest who caused his unjust ejection from his mission. While he thought this man would point him to the answer, Roger recognized that he was actually the root of his problem.

"Don't even get me started with food," Roger snapped.

"I worked at one of those fast food shops. It was a fried chicken joint. Man, I hated it there. They made me work as a cook. Like I can cook. Ha! I wanted to burn that place down. That's why I decided fast food wasn't for me. Yeah, I'm more of a white-collar man, if I do say so myself. Always enjoyed putting on a suit," Miles jabbered.

"Where's your suit now? We could've used some classiness back there," Roger said as he glanced at Miles' soiled clothes and greasy hair.

From his angle, he could see dirt crusted to Miles' ears from weeks without bathing. Roger looked down at his own clothes. "Look at me. I have no idea what the hell is going on. I'm tired, sick, I have nothing left!"

"Hey, don't fret my good man. Just be patient. You just need to move around. Get the blood flowing," Miles explained as he stood up.

Energy filled him as he pushed at Roger's back. "Come on now," Miles added, pressing harder.

Roger couldn't handle it anymore. Miles stayed beyond his welcome; in fact, he was never welcomed!

"No! Get away from me. Who the hell do you think you are? Huh? You have no job. You have no home. You're a bum, a hobo, a derelict! I have a life, a job…a wife," Roger exclaimed.

With his words, Roger lunged at Miles and threw his fist toward the pest's gut. Miles winced as the intended blow to his abdomen connected with his shoulder, knocking him back. Roger wobbled from the momentum. Miles grabbed Roger's shirt, tearing half of the buttons off the front and exposing his bruised chest. Roger's muscles rejected his abusive commands as he fell back toward the concrete. He grabbed at Miles to save his fall as his dangling fingers snatched a handful of Miles' oily hair. Roger's body bashed the concrete first, followed by Miles. The businessman let out a bellow as the breath blew from his lungs. Miles turned Roger around and kneeled on his back. In the flurry, the picture in Roger's back pocket flew out and landed on the ground.

Miles focused his attention on the image. He rolled off Roger's back and grabbed the photograph. Roger began violently coughing as his lungs wheezed for air. The winning victor, Miles, studied the couple staring back at him. He then looked in front of him at the frazzled man panting on the ground—his cut face, his torn clothes, and his bruised appendages. Miles glanced at the man in the picture. He wore a stylish polo shirt and shorts, his hair was parted on the side, and his skin radiated. Miles squinted as he wondered whether the man in the photograph was, in fact, the man now sitting in front of him. There was a slight yet definite resemblance to both men, particularly in the long face and distinct jaw. The man in the photograph had two dimples. Miles looked at the man sitting on the ground and realized he had never seen him grin. Roger combed his hair with his hands as he regained control. It was an instinctive reaction, ingrained in him from always looking his best. Miles widened his eyes as he saw the faint part in Roger's hair.

"That is the same man," Miles mouthed.

He wondered how this handsome and seemingly indestructible man went from riches to rags. Then, he asked himself the same question. Miles shifted his eyes to the bright and bubbly woman nuzzled close to Roger's side. She had a soft look that massaged even the most fatigued eyes. A grin formed on Miles' face as the woman entranced him.

"Who... Who is this?" Miles stuttered.

Roger calmed down, but his body throbbed even as he sat still. Miles' words didn't seem to faze Roger as he didn't want any more to do with the bum. He was trying to regain strength to run, or at least stumble, far away from him.

Maybe if I ignore him, he'll get the hint, Roger reasoned.

"Hey, this woman. Who is she?" Miles persisted.

Roger had no interest in amusing the man standing over him, but the mention of the word "woman" did raise his curiosity. Roger kept his head still and moved his eyes toward Miles. He saw that Miles was holding something in his hands. Then, Roger moved his head as Miles turned the image toward him. Roger enlarged his eyes, wondering how Miles had his photograph.

"That's mine. Give it back!" Roger barked.

"Who is she?"

"It's a picture of me and my wife."

Miles turned the picture back around. "Wow, she is beautiful. When was this taken?" he asked sincerely.

"Last year. I can still remember it," Roger said as he scooted toward a nearby trashcan.

He scrunched his brow as he used all of his energy to stand, trying to regain the only concrete item of the love of his life. Struggling, Roger fell back down to the pavement as his own body mocked him.

"Where is she now? What the hell happened, eh?" Miles curiously asked.

Roger lowered his head in confusion.

"That's what I'm trying to figure out. I think I was involved in that car crash last night," he explained.

"You think? Damn! You gotta get some help."

Miles suddenly felt overwhelmed with sympathy for his partner on the street. While he wished he had a better life, a life that didn't include sleeping on the street, it was all that he had known for years; it was a life he at least understood. But the man in front of him was very different. On the outside Roger appeared just like him, a wanderer without a clear purpose; however, the photograph he held between his fingers painted a much different picture.

"I can't get help. I already messed that up. It's a long story, but let's just say the law is after me. But I don't even care. I just want to find my wife. I need her... She—"

"Well, I think I found her," Miles said as he gave the picture back to Roger.

"Come on, I'm tired of your shit!" Roger yelled.

"No, she's famous!"

What's he talking about? Roger asked himself, figuring the pest had finally lost it.

Roger attempted to reposition his head, but the bones in his neck screamed. It was as if he had lost control over his body. He wondered if even another dose of medicine from the glass bottle would invigorate his body.

Roger finally mustered enough strength to look up at Miles. The drifter had his hand extended with his finger pointing at something across the street. Roger took a deep breath, knowing he had to move his head again to whatever object that had absorbed Miles. He figured it was something innocuous, an attractive woman swaying down the street or a streetwalker prowling for clients.

As Roger's eyes finally focused, he saw the flashing lights of several big screen televisions inside a home rental store.

What was Miles pointing at? Roger thought.

He didn't see anyone standing outside and the store itself was dark. On the television was an image of a woman in the corner of the screen with a newscaster addressing the camera. Roger squinted to see the woman, but as he strained, her picture filled the entire screen of the television.

The image on the big screen was that of a woman aged gracefully to thirty-six years. It was black and white, obviously a DMV-type photograph, but the woman depicted could catch any man's attention, regardless of color space. It was Lois Belkin, and her image was glowing on screen like a radiating flare shot into the sky.

Roger lifted his eyelids. He was speechless, motionless, emotionless. He couldn't believe the sight. It took a moment to register in his brain, but Roger finally realized the key to his daunting journey was just four lanes away. A jolt of electricity flowed through his body, bringing new life to his soul. It was as if he were in a new body, with his mind completely focused on the screen across the street.

Roger jumped up and darted across the busy road.

"Hey!" Miles yelled, completely blinded by Roger's burst of vigor.

A car slammed on its brakes, screeching to a halt as Roger hustled across the lanes, hurdling the pothole that had once fixated him. Another truck slowed and blared its horn, but none of the street's activity could stop Roger.

He reached the glass window and kneeled down on the sidewalk. Tears flowed down his cheek as the image of his wife glimmered off his watery eyes. Roger raised his hand to the glass and outlined her image with his fingers. Her smile, her dark, flowing hair, her supple skin, mesmerized Roger. He felt her presence surround him in the digital data swirling through the airwaves. The television captured the digital signal, which reflective mirrors from the projection television beamed to Roger's eyes.

Closed captioning flowed across the screen: "Police are asking for help with identifying any loved ones of Lois Belkin, age 36. She is recovering at Southern General Hospital from last night's horrific accident on Pleasant Place Bridge..."

The words "Southern General Hospital" caught Roger's attention as he blinked his eyes, regaining composure. Abruptly, he felt water drip onto his already soaked cheeks. Roger assumed it was his tears, but then he felt more drops hit the top of his forehead. He knew it couldn't have been tears. Suddenly, a flash of lightning overwhelmed the sky, followed by a burst of thunder.

Traffic had increased as Miles attempted to join Roger across the street. A truck whizzed by, sending the drifter back. The rain picked up as water pelted Miles' face. He saw a window of opportunity as he ran across the street, but then a sedan slammed on its brakes. Miles stopped. The car halted inches from his bones.

"Yo, can't you see I'm walking here!" Miles screamed as he banged on the hood of the sedan.

He continued toward Roger. Water began to pour down the store window, which distorted the television. Miles stopped behind Roger and looked in awe of her glow. Then, just like that, the striking image of Lois vanished on the screen.

"Hey, man. What did it say? Where is she?" Miles asked.

The rain had completely soaked through Roger's hair and clothes. His whole body couldn't escape the sky's tears. Another blast of thunder echoed through Roger, as he felt renewed and reborn. He turned in the direction of Southern General Hospital.

"That way, the hospital," Roger mouthed to Miles.

He was now a man on his ultimate mission, finally enlightened to the most important piece in his broken puzzle. Even with all of the missteps along the way, it was all worth it now. Roger figured he would not have seen the answer to his question had it not been for the spectacle at The Hideaway. While he had taken a step backward, he was now given the opportunity to take a leap forward toward the side of his awaiting wife.

Miles looked at Roger in astonishment. He could feel the energy ooze from him. Miles followed Roger's gaze as they stood in the cleansing rain.

Roger licked his lips. The rainwater tasted salty as it tinkled his dry tongue. Roger took a deep breath and whispered, "I'm coming."

19

The clock passed the three o'clock mark on the wall across from the nurses' station. Jennifer was busy at the computer with the doctors' notes from the day. She was the only nurse behind the front desk. Two other female nurses were making the rounds down the north and east wings. Nurse Ann was in the office behind Jennifer with another nurse, discussing her quarterly review. The final nurse on the shift was downstairs in the cafeteria on her break.

Jennifer came across a record on her spreadsheet application that was marked "Jane Doe." She remembered a memo from Nurse Ann regarding the nameless file. Jennifer dug around on the desk and found the message, which read to update Jane Doe's records with the name "Lois Belkin." She changed the fields in the computer document, and then found the paper file in the cabinet next to her. Using an ink pen, she crossed out the name and corrected it. Her next task was to make sure the computer file matched the paper file. She glanced at the "Injuries" category and compared the two formats. Both described the arm fracture to the right arm, internal bleeding that was now stabilized, and included the word "Coma" in bold letters. "Awaiting Neurologist Consult" filled the "Daily Update" field on the paper file, but was not included in the electronic version. As Jennifer typed the information into the computer, she realized that Lois was one of the victims of the horrific accident on the Pleasant Place Bridge. She finished updating the record and scrolled down farther until a particular field made her stop. The "Relatives" box was empty, as well as the "Emergency Contacts." The file resembled one for the homeless who had no family except for the streets.

"Excuse me," a woman's voice emitted, which startled Jennifer.

She looked up to see a middle-aged woman dressed in a large coat. Jennifer wondered why she hadn't heard the elevator ding through the stillness, but figured it was her preoccupation with Lois' file.

The middle-aged woman's presence jarred Nurse Ann's attention as she had a strategic view from her seat in the back office. The visitor was holding a tissue and dabbed her eyes as she focused on Jennifer. Nurse Ann peeked out of the back office. She wondered whether the woman was related to Lois, a "next of kin" in police lingo. The woman had a long face, red hair, and was short—barely over five feet tall. Nurse Ann tried to make out any resemblance to the sleeping beauty, but somehow she knew that the woman wasn't here for Lois. Nevertheless, the woman was obviously frazzled and Nurse Ann had a duty to help all those who sought information about the patients on her floor.

"Oh, I didn't see you there," Jennifer replied.

"I'm sorry to bother you, but my father, Edward Ulrich, was just admitted. He was in a car accident and the E.R. said he was here in recovery," the woman said through tears.

Nurse Ann walked from the office ready to assist the woman. She remembered her father's admittance to the floor several hours ago. He suffered numerous broken bones from a late night wreck, but his injuries were not life threatening.

Jennifer sprang from her seat. This woman was a high priority visitor who transcended normal visiting hours. This was something unique with her floor.

"I'll take care of it, Ann," Jennifer assured her boss.

"Yes, he's right this way. Please follow me," Jennifer responded as she put a compassionate arm around the weeping woman and walked her down to the north wing.

An eerie silence filled the nurses' station. Nurse Ann took in the stillness under the dim lights. The smell of soap invigorated her senses as she raised her head to allow more of the aroma to enter. She wondered where it had come from. Then her ears adjusted to the silence as the sound of ticking arose from somewhere. Her eyes shifted toward the source and focused on the clock on the wall. It read ten after three. The ticking made Nurse Ann focus on Lois. It was too quiet, as if the world had forgotten about the sleeping beauty.

Nurse Ann peeked into the office behind her. Her fellow nurse was busy reading through her proposed employee development plan, as required by the hospital.

"I'll be right back," Nurse Ann said to her.

She walked with quick steps down the west wing. She wanted to check on Lois and offer her a quick motivation to pull through her wakeless sleep. As she neared the room in the distant hallway, she saw two figures near the wall. They were shadowy with dark uniforms covering their obtrusive presence. At first, Nurse Ann quivered at the image, but then she remembered that these uninvited visitors were the two patrolmen who had interjected themselves on the floor. Nurse Ann had forgotten about them because she had been preoccupied with administrative tasks, but she had shivered with fear when they had first arrived just after eleven o'clock.

Nurse Ann remembered how the burly man had flashed his badge and told her of their orders from the city police captain. When Nurse Ann asked about Det. Cleveland, the scrawny patrolman scowled in disgust as his cohort reiterated the captain's order. She sensed trouble the moment both had clumped off the elevator. Their arrogant air as they moved, ogling the younger female nurses behind the station's desk, and their unwillingness to give her any information as to their intentions other than barking the word "captain" had worried her. Nurse Ann, however, knew their presence was related to Lois' husband Roger, the man she had never met. She felt such deep empathy for him and his journey. She sensed Roger nearby somewhere in the city, but she knew an army was searching for him. Nurse Ann hoped the one man on his side, and hers, Det. Cleveland, would reach Roger first. The detective had left her to embark on his mission with a look of determination, guided by only a city map and gut instinct. Nurse Ann prayed the detective would find Roger before any more tragedy could occur.

As she neared Lois' room, she could see the lugs perched on both sides of the door like pawns at a queen's feet. The husky man was engrossed in a magazine. Nurse Ann wondered what type of content might have pro-voked him, but his maneuvering of the magazine from horizontal to vertical plainly suggested that his interest lay in viewing pictures. His wide-eyed expression further confirmed that the images were probably not from *Good Housekeeping*. The skinny man had a blank stare as he bounced a rubber ball against the floor and caught it on its ricochet off the opposite wall. Nurse Ann reached Lois' room as the burly man remained engrossed in his picture spread while his friend glanced over and nodded. As their eyes locked, his hand still instinctively caught the springing ball, which suggested his supreme status in the sport of ball bouncing was likely gained from count-less hours of stake-out duty.

Nurse Ann pushed open the door as she heard the sound of Lois' heart. The room had a musty odor, which caused her to raise her head and direct her nostrils. She followed the smell to the open bathroom door. It was an unwritten rule on the floor to close the bathroom door in all of the rooms to contain any smells that could arise from leaky water pipes. As Nurse Ann swung the door closed, she peered back at the main door and shook her head at the obvious culprits to the room's odor.

Lois lay in her usual spot unchanged from the moment Nurse Ann had first seen her. While her com-plexion seemed a bit healthier, a bit more alive, Nurse Ann figured the softer lights were the reason. She placed her hand on Lois' face like a mother reaching for her ba-by. It seemed to feel warmer and more vibrant, but color and temperature fluctuated in those conscious and uncon-scious. Nurse Ann hoped the sleeping beauty's condition would change, as she knew that the more time that passed usually meant the coma was in place for the long haul. Lois just needed a familiar voice to awaken her, a voice from one she loved.

Nurse Ann leaned in to Lois' ear and whispered, "Don't worry, dear. I know you can pull through this. I'm sure those that truly love you are thinking of you right now."

20

The rain fell steadily over the early morning city. Darkness still engulfed the streets, but the morning commuters starting their workdays at dawn would soon fill the downtown with life. Several brave cars scattered the urban roads with their windshield wipers sloshing the water from their view. Det. Cleveland was one of those cars as he sat at a red traffic light mulling over the captain's misguided orders. He knew he should be traveling back to the precinct to offload all of the critical information he was collecting, but he knew it was a waste of time. As he sat at the traffic light, he studied his city map marked with areas to explore and areas already searched. The detective had spent over three hours driving the night streets searching for a man he didn't even know how to recognize.

Det. Cleveland glanced at the sign reading "Eighth Street." His eyes shifted from corner to corner hoping to find Roger. There were a handful of people roaming the water-covered streets, but they all had umbrellas and a place to go.

The rain had a hypnotic effect as it hit the sedan's roof. The water seemed to form a distinct pattern as it fell, yet it was undeniably random. The resonance, however, worked on Det. Cleveland as he attempted to discover the impossible pattern. He felt disconnected from the world as he sat alone at the red light, physically protected from the water, but still exposed in the middle of the street. His eyes focused on the burning red light, and his ears heeded the sound of water. As the rhythmic aura thickened around him, a cell phone pierced through it and caused Det. Cleveland to bounce in his seat.

"Cleveland here," he answered.

"Hey, it's me. You found anything out there, Ray? It's been hours," Charlie said.

"What do you got, Charlie?"

"I um…got some good news and some bad news."

Det. Cleveland's right hand man was sitting at his desk in the middle of the bustling police station. The precinct was overlapped with the graveyard shift personnel and several day shift employees called to start the day early. There was another reason, however, that sparked the flurry of officers, desk clerks, and administrative personnel. It was due to a high priority, or "hi-pri" case the law officers commonly abbreviated, that was currently developing within the precinct's jurisdiction. All cases had a codeword used to standardize the force's efforts, and this particular case was classified solely as "Belkin."

"What's the good news?" Det. Cleveland asked.

The traffic light turned green and the detective pulled out.

"Well, the good news is that I have Lois' sister, Carol, on the line. She just called in but she's pretty frantic," replied the researcher with a lukewarm tone.

"That's great news! Put her through," Det. Cleveland responded, widening his eyes.

He was excited to hear that a close family member had surfaced, as he wanted nothing more than to reunite the sisters. However, Det. Cleveland realized that Charlie had only completed half of his response, which made the excitement drop. What bothered the detective the most was not the fact that Charlie didn't give the bad news; it was the way he had delivered the good—lacking enthusiasm.

"Wait. What's the bad news?"

Charlie leaned in closer to his desk, a sign of something sensitive to come, something privileged. Even though Det. Cleveland couldn't see his confidant, he knew from years of working together that something important was to follow.

"Roger turned up again. This time he was thrown out of The Hideaway restaurant on Fourth Street about an hour ago. The manager requested an officer, and he described two men causing a commotion when our guys arrived. One matched Roger's description."

Charlie's words incited the detective. His focus shifted from the rainy street to the image of men tossing Roger out of their establishment. Then, a single word trumped the thoughts and images whirling around inside Det. Cleveland, "captain."

"Does the captain know?"

"Yes, and he wants him stopped. Said to take whatever means necessary. Ray, I think this guy better watch out. If you don't get him…well, I just don't want this to end badly."

Another light turned red. Det. Cleveland slammed on the brakes, preoccupied in the heat of the moment. The red traffic light burned into the cones of his eyes.

"God damn it, the captain is nuts if he thinks this guy is really dangerous. I mean, Christ, he was almost killed last night!" Det. Cleveland shouted. "Where is the captain anyway?"

"He's not here. He's at home."

"He's in his cushy bed and I'm driving these dark streets all night. He doesn't know what the hell is going on!" Det. Cleveland roared.

Charlie sat back and ground his teeth. He tried his best to delicately deliver the bad news, and he couldn't even imagine the emotions running through his boss' mind. Charlie wanted to make sure the detective knew that he was still on his side, as he would always be through thick and thin.

"I know. I know. I'm just telling you what's going on down here," Charlie replied.

Det. Cleveland gripped the steering wheel tightly. He felt like driving to the captain's house and barging in to argue the facts and to explain Roger's case. His logical mind, however, deduced that that would undeniably not help Roger. He might get to prove his point to the captain, make him realize a different viewpoint, the right viewpoint, but it did nothing for the imminent danger the lost traveler faced. The situation needed to be resolved on the streets, the place that no desk jockey could truly understand. If he was going to end this situation, he needed to do it now, and do it quickly. Through his fury, Det. Cleveland realized there was a hint of light in the darkness in the form of the good news.

"Do you still have Carol on the line?" he asked.

"Yeah."

"Put her through."

Charlie moved to patch her through, returning the silence. The rhythm of the rain calmed Det. Cleveland, massaging his rage into a manageable sensation. The water brought him back to the clarity he had felt at the previous traffic light. While the view at his stopped position on Tenth Street seemed similar to his previous stop, the red light appeared more intense. While it meant "stop" on the road, it didn't mean anything else. In fact, he didn't even have to stop. It was a law, but he was the law. Det. Cleveland looked up and saw the sign marked "Tenth Street" through the rain and recalled Charlie's words. He had mentioned a restaurant, a restaurant on "Fourth Street." Det. Cleveland glanced into his rear view mirror and punched the throttle. His tires spun as he whipped the car's tail around. As his engine roared through the night, the phone clicked again.

"Hello? Hello?" filled the detective's ears.

It was the sound of an overexcited woman. Carol had been patiently waiting to talk to someone, anyone. She had received the news by chance after a late-night flip of the television dial. Normally, Carol was a heavy sleeper who could snooze through the sound of a tractor-trailer's horn, but tonight was a restless night. Not speaking with her sister had made her mind uneasy, and an uneasy mind was one that didn't want to drift away to sleep. Just as importantly, not having her crutch, the man with whom she had vowed to spend her life, only added to the emptiness that had already overwhelmed her. These facts culminated in Carol tossing and turning through most of the night, which made her hand coast to the television remote. She remembered the feeling that was indescribable for anyone to receive. There, plastered on the main channel, was a picture of her sister. At first, she was in shock, curious about the reason for her sister's exposure, but then the newscaster explained the damning details. Her woman's intuition had proven correct. The knot that had tightened in her stomach as the day progressed had pained her for a reason. She grabbed a pen and pad and wrote down the phone number provided, as well as the location of her sister, "Southern General Hospital." Carol sprang from her bed and threw on a pair of sweatpants and a sweatshirt. Her dog, Lucy, aware of the danger, followed her closely until Carol reached the garage. As she jumped into her car, she dialed the number on her cell phone. Carol raced through the wee hours of the morning toward Southern General Hospital. The drive would take her about twenty minutes if the Pleasant Place Bridge was open. Fortunately for her, it was.

"Yes, ma'am. This is Detective Ray Cleveland. I am on your sister's case," Det. Cleveland replied as he sped through the rainy city.

"Oh, my God! I just saw the TV. I knew something was wrong."

It was not raining where she drove, but as she neared the lights of the city, she could see water pouring over the downtown.

"Where are you now?" he asked.

"I'm on my way to Southern General. Oh my God. Lois," Carol replied as she fought tears.

She was more energized than emotional, but the simple pronunciation of her sister's name caused her to cry.

Det. Cleveland juggled the phone as he sped down the street. He knew he should have engaged his police light, but following protocol took a backseat to "getting it done." He could hear the anguish in Carol's voice and wondered whether she sounded like the woman who everyone had sought to awaken. He felt electrified, free from the all-encroaching storm.

The Pleasant Place Bridge came into Carol's view. Its tall, ominous structure reached for the night sky as clouds consumed the top of its pointed suspension posts. As Carol took in the sight, she flinched as rain pounded her car's windshield. She was now entering a place that housed an isolated man with only a few allies.

The detective's voice commanded her attention. "Lois is on the fifth floor. Ask for Nurse Ann. She will take you to your sister."

Carol pressed the pedal farther and dodged the cars sprinkled on the early morning bridge. Her mind no longer pondered the location of Lois, and her journey to the hospital was the only obstacle that stood in the way of reuniting. As Carol passed the marred surface on the bridge from the accident, she realized the detective had failed to mention one crucial element of the situation, half of the situation, in fact.

"What about Roger? Is he okay?"

"Well, I'm working on that. He, well…he is on his way to see her," Det. Cleveland tactfully replied.

"Is he injured? Is he checked into Southern General?"

Carol's questions incited the detective even more. He suffered the same emotional charge that had energized Carol after hearing her sister's name. He dug his groomed nails into the leather-wrapped steering wheel and saw "Sixth Street" enter his view. Up ahead, the red light mocked him, but he didn't slow down. He kept his right foot pressed on the accelerator and hovered his left foot on the brake pedal. He darted his eyes left, and then right as he approached the intersection. Headlights emerged from the right.

The left foot or the right foot? he asked himself.

Then, almost without thinking, he firmly pressed a foot to the floor—the foot that sent his body back into the seat.

The encroaching car blasted its horn. Its tires locked. Det. Cleveland jerked the wheel to the left. Somehow, he cleared the car.

"Are you still there? Is Roger injured?" Carol repeated.

Det. Cleveland took a breath as he passed the "Sixth Street" hurdle.

"It's a long story. I will give you the details at the hospital. I'll be there as soon as I can. Just ask for Nurse Ann and only her. And be careful!"

"Okay, okay. Thank you," Carol replied as she passed the bridge.

She heard the click from the phone as she regained control of the wheel. Carol adjusted her wipers to the highest setting. Her view was cloudy, but at least her eyes were wide open.

21

Rain covered the city. The cars inched through nearly impassable streets. The drainage system at the corner of "Fourth" and "Broad" overflowed with water. Two valet drivers hid under the canopy of The Hideaway. They both stood silently, tired of chitchatting all night, and simply listened to the rain. It spoke in a rhythmic tone, but each object it hit resonated at a different frequency. It was like a game to discern the various noises, which occupied the young men's time when it had needed occupying. The two college-aged drivers had plenty of time on their hands as they eagerly waited until their shift ended at six o'clock. The taller of the two glanced at his watch, "4:12." This was the slowest time of the morning for the twenty-four hour establishment. Guests of the hotel were sound asleep and the restaurant crowd didn't know how to classify a meal. In addition, the rain had put an even bigger damper on potential patrons, but regardless of these variables, valet service was still a requirement.

Suddenly, the men heard the sound of a roaring engine. They watched as a sedan sped through the fierce rain. It neared the front of the entryway, and then its tires locked as the vehicle screeched to a halt. Both valet drivers looked at each other, thunderstruck. The car parked haphazardly with its tail end still hanging in the street. The door flew open as Det. Cleveland hopped out. He took a moment to take in the lights of the structure as the rain finally gave him its greeting. Water saturated Det. Cleveland's posh, water-resistant trench coat like a freshly squeezed sponge. He felt the energy of the establishment bathe him. The rainwater was salty. It was bizarrely refreshing, like a fully clothed jump into a pool. At the sight of the entryway, the detective hoped more answers than questions were inside.

He walked toward the front door. Both valet drivers were speechless.

"Don't park it! I'll be two minutes. Two minutes!" Det. Cleveland instructed.

He barged through the doors and stopped as his body adjusted. The cool, dry air aroused his senses. The doors shut behind him and the sound of the downpour vanished. As his pupils dilated, he looked toward the uninhabited hotel lobby, and then looked at the wall where Munch's *The Scream* glared at him.

What a disturbing painting, he thought.

Det. Cleveland shifted his focus to the restaurant entrance. He saw two figures dressed in black talking to one another near a podium. It was the familiar hostess and manager killing time just like their coworkers outside hiding under the canopy. These two, however, were not mute as their opposite sex chromosome sparked a primitive flirtation.

Det. Cleveland shook off his coat like a wet dog and grabbed his police badge. He slid toward the duo and overheard mumbled sounds that he was unable to formulate into English words; however, he did hear the word "breast" said by the man before both turned to the approaching figure in a trench coat. The badge did its trick as the polished silver glistened in the subtle light.

"Excuse me. I know you reported a disturbance earlier," the detective added to his badge's unspoken announcement.

"Yeah, I did. They said they were after one guy. He's in a lot of trouble," the manager said.

The manager took a deep breath at the sight of Det. Cleveland. It wasn't the type of breath inhaled due to fright, but it was the breath of anger, the breath the body required as it fired up. The manager recently spoke with two patrolmen dispatched about thirty minutes earlier. They were two different individuals than the two officers who were still stuck on stake-out duty at the hospital. It wasn't that the two men outside Lois' hospital room were the only officers available; in actuality, the captain had engaged a much larger force to handle the Belkin case. Officers were told throughout the city to be aware of the suspected felon.

The manager thought about his conversation thirty minutes ago. He explained the ruckus the apparent bum and his sidekick had made. Then he complained about how he had an unusual increase in vagrant activity over the past few days. The two dispatched police officers didn't seem to provide any insight into ways to curb the problem, as the patrolmen seemed solely interested in the details of one of the two drifters. It was the taller one with high-water pants as he referred to him, but little did the manager know, the man's name was Roger Belkin and he was currently the most sought after individual in the city. His suspicions would increase as Det. Cleveland unloaded even more questions on the strange man's whereabouts.

"Well, can you explain what exactly happened here?" Det. Cleveland asked.

"Yeah, the one guy came in demanding to speak to one of our waiters."

"Which man came in?"

The images of the uninvited visitors flashed back into the manager's mind. He remembered looking first at the hostess. She had a small but noticeable quiver to her lip and the crease between her eyebrows signaled duress. He remembered wondering what or who could have caused the normally bubbly girl to squirm, but then his eyes shifted to the man standing across from her. He had a peculiar look to him as his torn clothes, chaotic hair, and roughed face suggested weeks or even months of a hard life on the streets. Unbeknownst to the manager, the man was a prominent patron just the previous night. Regardless of Roger's true colors, the manager forcefully intervened and when his obtrusive counterpart, the weasel, burst through the doors, it was time to send in the infantry.

"It was the taller one, dark hair, wearing sloppy clothes. His pants were too short," the manager explained for the second time to the detective.

"And he was with someone else?" Det. Cleveland asked.

"Don't you police guys talk? Like I told the officers before, he had a friend, a short guy. Looked like a weasel, messy appearance, and yeah, he had a high-pitched voice," the manager continued.

Unaware to the manager, the police did communicate, but they didn't necessarily agree with one another's procedures. Just as a food server could choose to prioritize five tables in order of an anticipated tip, a police detective could make his own judgment in running an investigation. The chain of command in law enforcement usually settled disputes, but in this case, the detective was acting on his own intuition. He was the only savior that Roger, the misunderstood carjacker, misrepresented thief, and misclassified peddling bum, had in the city. The interesting tidbit to the detective was Roger's counterpart, a mystery man who seemed to be some form of a circus animal based on the descriptions given to him.

"Yeah, I remember the short one's voice. You can't miss him," the hostess added.

"What happened next?"

"The two wouldn't leave. They were very disruptive and were creating a scene in front of our customers. I'm trying to run a business here, you know," explained the manager.

"Do you know which way they headed?"

"Like I'm supposed to keep tabs on bums. They're probably playing in a dumpster for all I know," the manager said.

Det. Cleveland didn't appreciate the manager's quickness, but he didn't reveal his hand; he never did. The detective had skills to handle all sorts of individuals, ranging from gun-wielding criminals to obnoxious informants to even a deaf and mute robbery victim. Above all, he could read people as a doctor diagnosed an ailment, and he could see why this quick-tempered manager would call the police as a first response to a man who didn't walk in with a suit and tie.

The manager glanced at one of the muscular servers doubling as a bouncer to Miles and Roger's ejection. He was holding a plate of steaming Chicken Alfredo with Fettuccini Noodles high above his shoulder as the group caught his eye. The husky server was a man who liked his job as a waiter because of the interaction with guests, but the physical contact he had performed that early morning was not his favorite part of his unwritten duties. In fact, he had never worked in the security field, but his being pressed into service as a bouncer made him wonder whether that was a possible career path.

"Hey, come here a second," the manager said as he gestured to the busy man. "Do you know which way those two went?"

The server didn't lower his tray of Chicken Alfredo. Its heat was burning his palms and there wasn't any place to set the tray down.

"Yeah, they headed in the south direction. That way," he said, nodding.

He noticed the tall, prominent detective towering over his manager and knew he was a cop. This man, he figured, had to be on a different level than the men who had arrived about thirty minutes earlier. Their bold uniforms had proudly displayed the shield of the law, whereas this man seemed to blend into the night—a quality that he had surely planned.

"Thank you very much," Det. Cleveland responded as the server resumed his work.

The detective had the tidbit of information that he needed to continue. The south was not just a simple direction to move toward, like a meaningless coordinate in a treasure hunt; it meant something much more powerful. It was the direction of Southern General Hospital. Det. Cleveland was both delighted and nervous that Roger had found a sign that pointed him toward his wife. He was delighted that Roger seemed to be on his way to reuniting with his wife, but nervous that he was also nearing the trolls who guarded her.

Det. Cleveland turned with excitement, but he felt that his investigation in The Hideaway was not yet finished.

"Oh. One more thing. Do you still have the records for yesterday's reservations?" he asked the manager and hostess.

"Do you mean just a few hours ago or the day before?" she asked.

Det. Cleveland glanced at his watch and saw quarter past four in the morning.

"I mean the day before—about thirty-four hours ago," the detective clarified.

"Uh. Let me see," she muttered as she checked her records.

The manager watched on the sidelines, curious about the detective's intentions.

"Yes, here they are," she responded, grabbing the papers.

"Do you have a listing for Belkin?"

The name didn't register with the manager or the hostess. She skimmed the list using her index finger.

"Yes, Belkin, party of two. Seven o'clock," she read.

"Do you know who served them?"

"Yes. John. He's right over there," she responded.

Luckily for the detective, the waiter had begun a schedule change, which put him on during the early morning hours.

"What does this have to do with anything?" the manager asked.

Det. Cleveland ignored him, as he knew he was of no use anymore. The detective was focused on the waiter who had served the couple. He saw the server in the dining area and kept him in focus as he marched toward him, leaving the manager and hostess behind. As he walked into the tranquilly lit area, he slicked his drying hair back with his hands. There were only two couples dining. A man and woman in fashionable, yet borderline inappropriate, clubbing gear were seated at one table savoring their fresh Chicken Alfredo. The server named John took the order of an elegantly dressed couple. Det. Cleveland moved behind John as the couple looked at the slick man in a trench coat.

"I recommend the Italian dishes…" John added to his pitch.

"Excuse me," Det. Cleveland interrupted.

John, curious, turned as the detective flashed his credentials. "Do you remember serving a man and woman approximately thirty three hours ago?"

"Thirty three hours ago. When was that?" John asked.

"The night before last. About seven p.m.," Det. Cleveland explained. "The man was tall, had dark parted hair. She was wearing a black dress, had long dark hair."

"Well, I had a lot of customers," John said.

He had nearly a hundred guests on a good night and those descriptions could apply to many of them.

"Wine. They probably had wine. Lambrusco maybe," Det. Cleveland added.

Then, a light bulb went off inside John's mind. He remembered an attractive woman with a hint of feistiness in her expression as she ordered wine. She had a glimmer in her eyes when she looked at John, a hint that made him envious of the man sitting across from her. John remembered bringing them wine before their lasagna and spaghetti entrees.

"Oh yes, I remember them. They ordered Italian dishes."

"Did you notice anything out of the ordinary? Did they say anything that stood out?"

John remembered the moment that still swirls inside his mind.

"Yeah. It was their anniversary. He got her a necklace. They looked happy together. In love," John recollected with a smile.

Abruptly, John frowned as he wondered why this man of the law was inquiring about them.

"Why? What happened to them?" he asked.

Det. Cleveland grinned. "You just explained it all. Thank you."

The detective dashed toward the door, leaving John with a blank expression.

"Thank you for your help," Det. Cleveland said to the manager and hostess.

The liveliness in his movement was now vastly different from when he had entered. As he neared the glass doors, he took a moment to appreciate the calmness. Det. Cleveland knew that beyond that protective glass lay a much different world, a world consumed by a voracious rain and the site of his journey's last leg.

22

Silence filled the nurses' station on the recovery floor at Southern General Hospital. Jennifer was still on the computer as her other four colleagues prepared a cart for the morning medication run. Nurse Ann was somewhere on the floor, although the five nurses didn't know exactly where she was. The nurses worked in the stillness as their soft shoes shuffled on the hard floor like feathers painting the ground. Even though their gentleness and grace had failed to generate noise, the faint sound of the tremendous rain mesmerized them. It was low and distant, but provided those out of its path with a sense of relief for the protection of a physical structure. Suddenly, a thunderous boom vibrated the building. Jennifer stopped and focused on the storm's sensations. A flowerpot near her chattered on the counter, powerless to the thunder.

A ding from the elevator sounded, jarring Jennifer's attention. Something about it sounded unusual. It sounded more prominent and rawer than normal like a shriek of terror. Jennifer watched the silver door, anticipating the person who filled its confined space. Then, it opened. Jennifer's gaze fell on a frantic face covered by water-soaked hair. It was Carol.

Lois' sister took in the openness on the recovery floor. The mess of the bustling entryway was the opposite of her new space. The incredible rain brought in more business for the hospital, a business that paradoxically didn't want new clients. Carol had barely received a response from the flurrying first-floor information desk, and only after raising her voice did they direct her to the fifth floor. But now, Carol was in a much different world.

Jennifer stood up when she saw Carol.

"Uh, Lois Belkin. I'm her sister. Do you know where she is?" Carol asked frantically.

Her words roused the attention of the other four nurses. They all remained silent for a moment trying to digest not only the words, but Carol's frenzied delivery. Jennifer began to gesture toward Lois' room, but a voice cut her off, "Right this way, dear. I'm Nurse Ann."

Nurse Ann emerged from the side hallway and gravitated toward Carol. She gestured for her to follow and shook Carol's trembling hand on their way to the west wing. They moved quickly through the long hall-way like water racing through a broken dike.

"Oh God, I just found out about her. She was just out for her anniversary. This wasn't supposed to happen," Carol quivered.

Nurse Ann put her hand on Carol's back. The truth was out in the open, and Carol's voyage to her sister's side was almost over.

"I know this has all been very strange, but your sister is in good hands."

Both turned the corner. While nearly fifty identical doors stood shut on both sides of the hallway, the sole door with two officers outside it drew Carol's attention. She hoped their presence was for a different patient, but as Nurse Ann headed toward the door, Carol realized they were guarding the room that housed her sister.

"Why are *they* here?" Carol asked.

"It's a long story."

The two patrolmen sat up, curious about the new visitor. The men didn't speak; they only watched. Nurse Ann pushed open the door. Carol paused between the two patrolmen like a commoner standing before a guarded queen. She was afraid to enter, terrified of confronting the condition of its occupant. Carol hoped to hear Lois' familiar voice. However, Carol didn't hear anything, only the eerie electronic beep of a beating heart. The heartbeat remained constant and unchanged, which further raised Carol's level of anxiety. Then, as the group stood in silence, a muffled yet distinct sound revealed itself—the sound of pouring rain.

Nurse Ann held open the door as Carol widened her eyes to behold a sight that she could never have imagined. Her sister, the princess of the family, lay in the center of the tranquil room awaiting her prince. A cast and sling were positioned on her right arm resting on her side. Her other hand was positioned on top of the tight covers, lightly draped on her abdomen. Her hand moved faintly up and down as her lungs involuntarily filled with the cool, dry air. Carol gravitated without speech and without thought toward her sister.

"Oh, Lois," she mumbled.

Carol placed her hand on Lois' face. It was soft and warm, which puzzled Carol, but then she realized it probably felt that way because her own hand was cold. The constant beep echoed next to her ear as she watched her sister's inanimate face starved of any outward life.

Nurse Ann watched on the side as the two sisters bonded. She looked at Carol's hand petting her sister's cheek. The added color to Lois' face absorbed Nurse Ann, as the comatose woman seemed healthier and more alive than she had previously remembered. Then, she heard the sound of sobbing. It was much more intense than a normal cry as only a deep emotional burst could produce Carol's gasping and rocking body. Nurse Ann walked over and placed a compassionate hand on Carol's back, offering her touch as comfort.

"She arrived last night from the crash. I guess you heard that. Well, her condition is stable. Aside from a broken arm and some bumps and bruises, we are just waiting for her to wake up," Nurse Ann explained.

"When will she wake up?" Carol asked through her tears.

"You can never tell with these things. Sometimes it takes days or weeks, but I do know that having family nearby helps significantly. They say that your sense of hearing still works even if you're in a coma," Nurse Ann said as she watched the sorrow in Carol's face. "I'm sure now that her sister is here, she will have something to wake up for."

Nurse Ann pushed a chair to the side of the bed. Carol sat down without taking her gaze from her sister. She leaned in close to kiss Lois' forehead as her nostrils received a hint of an unforgettable aroma, her sister's natural scent. It massaged Carol's emotions and triggered a burst of memories to flow through her mind—Lois greeting her at the front door, her sister wearing a summer sundress during an afternoon shopping trip, the sight of Lois nuzzling Roger at a cocktail party. Just as quickly, the pictures regressed in time as Carol remembered running as a young girl through a summer night's rain with the six-year-old Lois following closely. Carol felt like she was back at that night, the older sister leading the way through the water. Unexpectedly, the images vanished. Her sister's laughter and full-of-life expression was now replaced with a stillness that she had only witnessed during Lois' sleep. But this sleep was such that even the hand of a loved one could not wake. Carol wondered whether Lois was waiting to awaken for that one person who held the key to her heart, Roger. While Lois' dilemma lay in front of her, Roger's absence was even more frightening. Carol knew that Roger stood by Lois' side the last time she had spoken to her sister, but now, only an empty space was next to her.

"Where is Roger? Is he here?" Carol asked.

"Well, he, uh…" Nurse Ann hesitated.

"What?"

Through the silence, Carol glanced back at the door where the two patrolmen were perched. A sudden chill traversed her body as Nurse Ann's dithering could only mean something negative.

A flash of lightning bounced into the room, catching the women's attention. Quickly, a crash of thunder chased it. Nurse Ann stared out the window as her voice echoed inside the hospital room, "A good police detective is on his way. He will fill you in."

23

A boom of thunder ricocheted through the tall downtown skyscrapers. Rain blanketed the bustling city streets as traffic exponentially increased with the morning rush nearing. Full darkness still consumed the downtown with the barrier of clouds and rain giving the approaching sunrise a losing battle.

Roger charged through the rain, which pelted his face. He kept his head up as he traveled in the direction of his wife. Miles tried to keep pace, but the lack of food inside his belly made his muscles fail. Although Roger lacked any sort of tangible caloric intake just like his friend, he was acting not on stored energy, but on stored love. A gust of wind punched Roger's right shoulder. He spun around and bounced off a metal trashcan. The opportunity allowed Miles to gain some ground.

"Hey! It's horrible out here! Shouldn't we take cover? Wait till this blows over?" Miles yelled through the rain.

Roger kept moving, but the right side of his stomach pained him. At first, he assumed it was his hungry gut, but the throbbing seemed external and concentrated on his right side. Roger glanced down at his shirt and saw the deep color of red saturating the already rain-drenched fabric.

"Hey! Are you okay?" Miles asked.

Roger raised his shirt and saw a one-inch gash on his abdomen. The puncture was deep, splitting apart all layers of skin, but the rainwater washed away the blood making it appear less severe. Nevertheless, the wound required medical attention and added even more damage to his already damaged body. Roger tasted the rain and looked in the direction of his final destination.

"I have to get to my wife. I need her, and she needs me."

"I hear you, my man. But you can't fight Mother Nature, my daddy always said. Too bad we don't have a car. Damn, I wish I had my old beater. She would've got us there, no problem."

A truck splashed water on Roger's feet as he looked toward the morning traffic. Miles' logic made sense, Roger figured, as finding a vehicle would shave off time from the uphill journey. Roger darted into the traffic like a toddler chasing a rolling ball. He eyed a dark SUV traveling through the rain. It was tall, wide, and painted jet black. As Roger stared at the approaching headlights, he realized it was the same model he owned—at least until the accident. The lights headed closer and closer as Roger recognized the vehicle might not stop. Either way, he was unable to move, unable to dive for cover in case the SUV failed to halt. He had made up his mind to flag down a vehicle. Abruptly, Roger heard the squeal of rubber sliding across the water-coated tar. The SUV stopped as Roger felt a gush of rain fly from the hood.

Roger moved around to the driver's side as the window rolled down halfway.

"Excuse me," Roger said to the shadowy interior.

"Are you nuts? I almost hit you!" the driver's deep voice barked.

Roger saw the beady eyes of a muscular African American businessman dressed in a suit.

"Whoa! Whoa!" Miles screamed to the cars behind the stopped SUV. He had followed Roger into the street and was now acting like a traffic cop.

"Can I borrow your car? Or, uh, I mean can you give me a ride?" Roger asked the infuriated businessman.

"Man, you're crazy! What're you on?"

Unbeknown to Roger and Miles, a police car had stopped several cars behind the stalled SUV. Its occupant was a cop patrolling the streets looking for the "hi-pri" man, Roger Belkin. The patrolman raised his neck as he attempted to discern the hold-up ahead. Through the murkiness, he saw the figure of a short tousled man, a bum he reasoned, standing in the middle of the road directing traffic. Instinctively, he engaged his red and blue lights and flipped his siren.

Roger heard the unmistakable siren wail and looked in its direction. He saw the raindrops dispersing the vivid red and blue lights of a vehicle that was undeniably a police car. Both Roger and Miles scurried back toward the sidewalk as a passing vehicle in the oncoming lane hit its horn.

The black businessman punched the throttle; his SUV launched forward.

The patrolman saw the duo hustling down the sidewalk, one short and one tall. He remembered the call from the dispatch informing him and his fellow officers to look out for a parade of two bums, one short and one tall, the tall one being the wanted Roger Belkin.

"Hey! Stop! Both of you!" the patrolman yelled over his loudspeaker as he nailed the gas and sped toward the fleeing couple.

Several blocks away, Det. Cleveland raced through the heavy traffic toward the hospital. He drove erratically, seatbelt unfastened and trench coat partly hanging out of his driver's side door, as he scanned the streets in search of Roger. The city map lay crumbled on the floor of the passenger's side as his stop at the restaurant had significantly lowered his search radius. The answer to Roger's location was now up to his eyes. His eyes, however, were filled with gloom and blaring headlights. As the detective monitored the unclear sidewalks, a voice cut in on his police radio.

"Attention all units, we have two suspects on foot at First and Poplar heading south in the direction of Southern General Hospital. One fits the description of Roger Belkin wanted for Grand Theft Auto and in connections to Retail Theft. All units are asked to assist. Take any and all precautions as the suspects are assumed to be armed and dangerous."

Det. Cleveland widened his eyes and pressed his right foot farther to the floor. He knew he was running out of time as the city's army focused their might on the misunderstood man. He attempted to navigate the downtown road, but the heightened traffic prevented his full speed maneuvering.

"Come on! Move!" he commanded.

Det. Cleveland glanced at the center console and realized he had a solution underneath his right elbow. He unearthed a red police light mountable to the roof of a vehicle. The light rarely saw any use, but at this point, he needed something to make a passageway through the wall of traffic. While the detective usually relied on stealth rather than force, now was a time that force was the only option. He lowered his window halfway as the rain poured into the car's open wound, which further doused his already soaked trench coat. Through the wind, Det. Cleveland flipped a switch, which engaged the red rotating light. At first, he could not tell if the light actually worked, but a stubborn truck in front moved to the right and slowed. With that problem solved, he pegged the gas, as his car's speed was now his only barrier to reaching the hospital.

24

A bolt of lightning ignited the sky as a thunderous boom immediately followed. Roger hiked down a sidewalk toward a cross street. Miles was several paces behind, but fully energized from their near hit with the police. They lost the police car not by speed or stealth, but by the overpowering rain and its ability to conceal everything under its wrath. Roger recognized his location and knew that as he reached the approaching cross street, his journey would end. He battled the howling wind, but saw the street ahead coming closer and closer. Finally, he turned the corner and paused as he saw...it.

Southern General Hospital towered under the torrential rain. Its red cross shined on the top of the building like the North Star for weary travelers.

Two figures moved through the blinding rain. They were barely recognizable, like scurrying ants lost in a mound of dirt, but their insignificant presence was still distinguishable. It was Roger and Miles moving toward the tremendous structure.

The wandering businessman no longer needed to wander, as the end was in front of him. A wall of rain was the only thing standing between him and his wife, an obstacle he was prepared to overcome. As he crossed the street toward the hospital parking lot, a sudden sound overtook the rain. It was the sound of an approaching siren. As his ears filled with the impending force, he realized it was not the noise made by only one siren, but by an army of them. The noise intensified and surfaced in front of him as well.

"Hey! Wait up!" Miles yelled at his accomplice, who was surging ahead. All at once, Miles' eyes filled with the sight of red and blue lights spinning from all directions. He watched as Roger did not flinch.

The enraged police cars spun into the parking lot from all entrances, encroaching on the two men. Roger plowed through an ankle-high puddle of water as he saw the hospital's entryway emerge thirty yards away.

Roger's heart pounded inside his chest. His lungs gasped for oxygen as he pushed himself to the limit. His mind was solely focused on his wife, the woman unjustly torn from him. Three police cars squealed to a stop behind Roger, but it didn't matter; the last thing he was going to do was look back. Infuriated officers burst from each car armed with nine-millimeters and arteries full of adrenaline.

"Stop!" yelled one officer, wielding his weapon.

"Freeze! I said freeze!" screamed an irate female officer.

The officers eyed Roger's body through the rain as they covered him from all angles with their water-resistant weapons. Roger, however, did not recoil. He saw the bright lights of the hospital interior only a few more steps away. It looked pure, safe, almost heavenly. Suddenly, two figures emerged through the automated door. They stole the luster from Roger's view. At first, he thought they were benign, but the glistening object pinned on the skinny one's chest hurt Roger's eyes. It was the badge of the city police department. The two patrolmen dispatched to guard Lois headed his way.

Roger kept moving, but he watched as both men wielded their pistols. In an instant, his mind instinctively instructed his body to cease its drive, to kill its raging motor. As he stopped dead ten feet from the entryway, he realized he had nowhere to turn. His stationary motion caused the rain to change from horizontal to vertical as it covered his body. Roger remained perfectly still, but his eyes took in the reflection on the entryway's glass. He saw the army of police surrounding him. Roger was terrified to turn around, wishing desperately to make the last several steps to see the love of his life. He wished there were an easy way to explain his predicament and his daunting journey, but there were no words to explain it.

"Now turn around, slowly!" instructed an officer with his hand resting on his gun's trigger.

An odd silence filled the area as the sound of the rain resonated. A crowd gathered. Without warning, bystanders screamed.

"Hey! Let him go!" Miles exclaimed as he attempted to stick up for his fellow comrade.

"Down! Get down on the ground!" an officer commanded.

Miles wavered and dropped to the ground. He tried his best to help, but his best was worthless.

Roger stood all alone, isolated in his own world. He slowly turned to face his accusers as he witnessed the army following him.

"This is wrong. This is all wrong," Roger reasoned.

"Stay there!" the officer instructed.

Roger closed his eyes. He removed himself from the cancer and focused on the circle of light in the darkness. He was so close. He wanted to take the last few steps; he needed to. Roger opened his eyes to confront the army, but something that he could never have expected surrounded him. The enraged officers all stood motionless, regressed from pit bulls to beagles. Their guns were lowered; their boisterous voices were silent; their faces were blank like puppets. Roger spun around as everyone simply stopped and stared. Even Miles stood stone-faced. The only movement was the revolving red and blue lights through the pounding rain. It was as if everyone had realized Roger's journey, his journey into the darkness, and now they would stand in front of him no more.

Roger walked past the dozen blank officers. He stepped past the two patrolmen at the hospital door, and then entered the castle. Stillness consumed Roger. Nurses stopped and stared. A janitor watched while holding his mop. And even patients still in their gurneys sat up and stared as if Roger were a saint.

The businessman's shoes sloshed on the tile as he moved toward the elevator. He neared the reflecting metal doors, and then a ding sounded. The elevator opened as if it too were waiting for Roger. He stepped inside as the lift brought him to the fifth floor, all without Roger doing anything.

The doors opened. Roger stepped out as a deserted floor greeted him. He saw the lights illuminated down only one of the three hallways. Roger followed the lit path. He passed closed doors on each side and continued through the light. Roger turned the corner, and stopped as he saw the trail leading to the only open room. Even though he had no map, he knew exactly who was inside. Roger staggered down the hall, each step wider and stronger. He sensed the presence of the woman he craved, the woman he loved more than anything. Roger's breathing shuddered. Tears filled his eyes. Each step brought him even more emotion. And then, he stood in the doorway.

Roger fought his tears as his pupils adjusted to the soft light inside. Then, he took one more step, the last step into the room. He saw a figure in the bed. Roger crept closer as the sweet scent of his love invigorated him. He neared his wife as her soft, supple skin glistened and massaged his eyes.

"Lois. I made it," Roger whispered.

He inched closer, overwhelmed with emotion. But then, something stole his focus. It was the torrential rain outside the window. A blast of thunder erupted. A bolt of lightning flashed. Roger closed his eyes. After a moment, he opened them and saw the face of a man covered with rage. Roger spun around and saw an army of police. He realized that he was back outside, back to reality, and gone from his wife's side.

Roger took a breath. He had to find a way out. His mind yelled, and then a sudden, enlightening feeling overwhelmed him. He saw a solution to his problem, a solution that he hoped would explain his situation to those around him. Roger reached slowly into his rear pocket. As his arm moved behind him, the officers stood tall and reaffirmed their weapons.

"Don't move! Stop!" erupted from the army.

"Put your hands up! Stop or we'll shoot!" another exclaimed.

Roger, however, felt calm. He knew the answer was in his back pocket as he prepared to remove the item that he hoped would explain it all.

"I just… I just want to see my dynamite," Roger explained as he reached deep inside him.

"Dynamite? Bomb! I think he has a bomb!" exploded from the chaotic crowd.

Their yells and screams frantically filled the area.

Roger smiled as he began to remove his hand, but then a quick flash and blast filled his senses. At first, he thought it was a jolt of lightning and thunder, but the sudden pain in his chest diverted his focus. He looked down as his smile turned into a look of terror. The front of his shirt had two small holes. Suddenly, the holes turned deep red, the color of blood. Roger realized the flashes had not been produced by the storm, but instead by the pistols of his aggressors. He had been shot twice in his chest. One bullet was embedded into his right lung as the other had broken heart.

"Noooo! Holster your weapons!" Det. Cleveland yelled as he ran into the middle of the action.

He finally reached the man, the man he had grown to understand, the man he had vowed to protect. His arrival, however, was seconds too late. Most people failed to appreciate the significance of a few seconds, but it was a measure of time that fit many facets of life—a sudden sneeze, a stubbed toe, or the moment of death. Det. Cleveland realized that a matter of seconds would haunt him for the rest of his life, as he could do nothing now to help Roger. He could only watch the life leave his beaten body.

Roger looked out and stared at the nearly one hundred police and bystanders frozen in silence. They stood stock-still; the only motion was that of the rushing raindrops. Roger blinked his eyes rapidly as the pain intensified deep within his chest. It felt like an uncontrolled tractor-trailer had run over his heart. The feeling was so intense that it lacked feeling. He attempted to turn in an effort to complete his journey, but his legs didn't respond. He realized they no longer worked. Roger fell to the ground on his knees. He looked down at the once light-colored shirt and saw it was now soaked with blood. Roger felt the bullets sucking the life from him, and he knew this was it. As the rain hit him, he recognized that he would never complete his journey, never step into the hospital and reunite with his wife. Roger felt his head bobble and fall forward as his neck muscles died. His breathing slowed. His pupils dilated. His muscles shut down.

An odd memory surfaced in Roger's mind. It was of his last conversation with his dying grandfather many years ago. Roger was only twelve at the time, but he could recall that memory as if it were yesterday. His grandfather had said, "As the years go by filled with life, one sometimes assumes his place in this world is infinite. If he took a moment, however, to fathom the number of years the Earth has spun in the infinite universe, he would realize those years of his life were nothing more than an insignificant raindrop produced by a violent storm that encircled the world."

The last image Roger would ever see was in front of him, an image every human life would see one day. For him, it was a puddle of water. His fading body reflected back as he saw himself dying, an image he could never have imagined, but there it was, directly in front of him. He was scared, realizing this was the end. Death was inevitable, which all living creatures must face on their day, but what Roger feared most was the unknown, the transition into a place, a time, and a state that no living creature could possibly comprehend. As he accepted his fate, the vivid image of his wife flashed before his eyes. Her soft radiating skin, her flowing brown hair, and her glowing smile were a part of him that would, and could, never die. Rapidly, Roger's eyes clouded. The image of the puddle blurred. He could not move, and he could not breathe. He attempted to inhale a gulp of air, but he could not. Roger suddenly felt trapped and unable to fill his screaming lungs. It was the most horrifying feeling he had ever experienced. Every second seemed like an eternity as he felt completely alone. Nothing or no one could possibly understand his state, but he realized that eventually we all would experience this unavoidability. It was just a matter of time. In a flash, the pain subsided and a burst of light filled his eyes. An emotional charge traversed through his mind, his body, and his soul. It was the feeling of bliss. Then through the blinding light, he heard something so vivid, so bizarrely familiar. It was the sound of a—

Det. Cleveland watched as Roger's dead body bashed against the ground. Water splashed into the air from the force. Roger lay perfectly still on the ground. The detective rushed toward him and grabbed the item that Roger had attempted to display. He picked it up and showed the stunned crowd.

"A picture, God damn it! He had a picture. Dynamite is his wife! He had a damn picture! He was just trying to find his wife!" Det. Cleveland screamed as he moved around the crowd.

The stunned group of police and bystanders surrounded Roger's departed body, completely immobile and unable to digest the chain of events. Det. Cleveland kicked a puddle of water as he held the rain-soaked picture in his hand. He realized he had lost and, although the man he had so desperately sought was right in front of him, he was face down and dead in the water like a belly-up fish.

25

Lois lay perfectly still in her comatose state sleeping through the battle outside the castle. Carol sat beside her holding her hand with the door propped open to circulate the air. The sudden departure of the two perched patrolmen had stirred Carol's attention; however, her focus was and would always be on her sister. She would not leave her side until she did all that she could to bring Lois out of her seemingly wakeless sleep, and even then she would keep trying.

Nurse Ann had left the room to let the two sisters reunite. In fact, the nurse encouraged Carol to talk to her sister in the hopes of awakening the tranquil woman from her trance. Carol did just that, softly petting her sister's hand and massaging her ears with her familiar voice. Carol also realized that her sister could stay sleeping for months, even years, which seemed horrifying to consider. The moments alone with Lois allowed Carol to examine her sister. She studied Lois' perfect hairline rounding her face, her small, creased chin, and subtle nose flares from her involuntary breathing. Carol counted the tiny eyelashes lined up on Lois' closed eyes, but in a sudden flash, she noticed a twitch under her eyelids. At first, she questioned the quiver, but convinced herself it did actually occur. She wondered whether such an occurrence was normal.

Carol realized something changed in the hypnotic sound hitting her ears. It wasn't the electronic monitor as Lois' heartbeat remained constant and rhythmic over the course of her stay. The subtle difference had occurred outside. The sound of the rain had stopped, which the continual electronic beat next to her masked. No longer was the howling wind, pelting rain, random booms of thunder, or flashes of lightning present. Carol stood up and walked toward the window, curious to see what her ears had deduced. As she neared the drawn blinds, she noticed a hint of light through the cracks. Carol parted the blinds. Her eyes filled with the emerging sun through the distant buildings. Without warning, the electronic heartbeats changed tone; the constant tempo escalated and began to resonate random notes.

Carol saw her sister's eyes rapidly moving under her lids. Her left arm twitched slightly, and her toes fluttered.

"Lois. Can you hear me? Come on, sis," Carol said as she squeezed her hand.

Lois moaned and whimpered under her breath.

"Nurse Ann! Nurse Ann!" Carol yelled.

Lois attempted to open her eyes, but they seemed to shudder randomly.

"Yes, baby. It's your sister. You can do it."

Finally, the princess opened her eyes wide as her pupils flexed from the light. Regaining her orientation, she focused on her sister's tears.

"What... Where am I?" Lois asked.

Before Carol could answer, Nurse Ann burst into the room and widened her eyes at the awakened woman. She ran to Lois' other side and rubbed her legs through the sheets with excitement.

"I'm your nurse, dear! You made it through!"

"You were in an accident, honey. But you're okay now," Carol added.

Lois registered the two women's enthusiasm. She glanced at her right arm covered in a cast. It was all puzzling. She had a deep throbbing from within her brain as her mind caught up to her body. The words hitting her ears didn't fully click, but one did stand out.

"Accident?" Lois repeated.

"Yes. You and Roger were driving home from dinner last night. Remember? It was your anniversary," Carol said.

"Actually, the night before last," Nurse Ann clarified as the sunrise peered through the window and warmed her face.

"Do you remember that?" Carol asked.

Lois studied her sister's face, but everything was a blur. The moments before her awakening were lost in a void. She felt like she had been gone for years, unable to remember falling into the sleep from which she had just awoken.

"No. I, uh, don't know," Lois unsteadily replied.

Slowly, she digested Carol's words as her brain regained control. She realized some sort of event had put her in the hospital. The excited nurse, beeping heart monitor, and tight cast all proved her plight, but something that Carol mentioned rose to the top of her mounting questions.

"Roger? Where is Roger?" she asked as she searched for him in the room.

Lois yearned for her husband, her partner, her crutch. Carol and Nurse Ann remained mute. Their silence concerned Lois, as she hoped to hear that he was just down the hall on his way to reunite with her, but these words didn't echo inside the confined room.

Suddenly, a warm masculine voice startled the trio, "He didn't make it."

Lois tried to place the faceless man, as she recognized it wasn't the familiar voice of her husband, her Roger.

"What?" she responded.

Det. Cleveland stepped into the room and stood at the foot of the bed, completing the circle surrounding Lois. His outward expression was unreadable and aloof; however, he felt overwhelmed with deep emotion. He had witnessed something that would change his life forever and now it was his duty to deliver the dreaded news.

"He died in the accident, trying to save you," he said tenderly.

Carol and Nurse Ann felt a chill run through their bodies. The only thing they could do was hold on to Lois tightly and never let go. Det. Cleveland removed the item Roger had carried with him throughout his journey, the picture of the loving couple. It was still wet from the rain. He placed it softly on Lois' chest like a petal that gracefully fell from a dying flower. Lois looked at the image as her world suddenly crashed. She realized she had awoken to a different world, a world where love no longer existed.

"Roger loved you very much," Det. Cleveland whispered as he held Lois' legs through the covers.

The detective watched her as she studied the picture with a blameless gaze. A deep flow of sensation overwhelmed him as the thought of Roger's journey pierced his emotional shield. His typically logical and unaffected mind was no match for the subjectivity of life and love. Det. Cleveland was a changed man and would never be able to go back to the way things were before he started the case. A tear formed in his eye and held for a moment on his lower eyelid teetering like an overfilled glass of water. Then, it trickled down his cheek.

"Oh, Roger. I love you…" Lois mumbled.

Tears poured down her face, as she could not think of anything else other than her loving husband. She thought of him sitting behind his prominent desk in his office, his nonchalant sway as he walked to her after a day's work, and his soft voice mouthing the word "dynamite" when she energized him with her feistiness. The forgetful man could never be forgotten, as he would always be just as she remembered him.

Lois held the rain-soaked picture snugly as a droplet of water slid down her arm through the open crease of her gown and rested over her beating heart.

Nurse Ann, Carol, and Det. Cleveland clutched Lois tightly and bonded with her as one over Roger's quest driven by undying love. They held on to her and would never relinquish their grip.

Outside the hospital, the sun had risen over the distant skyscrapers and bathed the city in warm light. It burned out the rain clouds as a beautiful and vivid rainbow cast over the energized city.

About the author:

Jonathan Sturak grew up in the Pocono Mountains of Pennsylvania. He is a Penn State University graduate and holds degrees in Computer Science and Film. He currently lives in Las Vegas where he uses the energy of the city to craft stories about life and the human condition. *The Place Called Home*, Sturak's essay about Eastern European heritage in Northeast Pennsylvania, was featured on *Glass Cases*, associate literary agent Sarah LaPolla's pop culture blog at glasscasesblog.blogspot.com. Sturak is also a contributing editor at NoirNation.com, the premier location for international crime fiction. His debut thriller novel *Clouded Rainbow* was published in December 2009 and has over 100,000 downloads on the Amazon Kindle. New for 2013 is his crime thriller novel *Vegas Was Her Name* published by Noir Nation Books. Sturak keeps updated information on his website at sturak.com